Come Away

Come Away

Song of Songs

ANNE HINES

McArthur & Company
Toronto

First published in Canada in 2007 by
McArthur & Company
322 King St. West, Suite 402
Toronto, ON
M5V 1J2
www.mcarthur-co.com

Library and Archives Canada Cataloguing in Publication

Hines, Anne, 1958-
Come away : Song of songs / Anne Hines.

ISBN 978-1-55278-635-2

1. Bible. O.T. Song of Solomon--Fiction. I. Title.

PS8565.I63C64 2007 C813'.54 C2007-900234-X

Design and Composition by Tania Craan
Printed in Canada by Friesens

The publisher would like to acknowledge the financial support of the Government of Canada through the Book Publishing Industry Development Program (BPIDP) and the Canada Council for our publishing activities. The publisher further wishes to acknowledge the financial support of the Ontario Arts Council for our publishing program.

10 9 8 7 6 5 4 3 2 1

For my mother,

Otha Sim

Who taught me to think for myself.
And, who has graciously lived with the consequences.

I wish to extend my sincere thanks to the following for their kind assistance with the researching of this book:

Grant Frame, Library of Royal Inscriptions, University of Toronto,
Sandra Harding,
Jack Howard, Royal Ontario Museum,
Larry Pfaff, Art Gallery of Ontario,
J. Glen Taylor, Wycliffe College, University of Toronto,
Peter Wyatt, Emmanuel College, University of Toronto.

Also to
My editor, Beth Follett
Rick Mugford for sharing his invaluable talent for detail
Ina Bogusz, Cheryl Glassman and Scott White
Generous patron of the arts, Michael Hines
Kim McArthur and the wonderful staff at McArthur & Co.
who continue to offer me such generous support.

And
Liz Earley and Keltie Sim, my twin pillars.

Arise my love, my fair one
And come away
For lo, the winter is past
And the rain has fallen
The flowers return to earth
The time of singing is come.
Arise my love, come away.

Song of Songs
Holy Bible

Come Away

I
537 BC

The Tigres River flows down toward the scorched plains of Syria, past bustling farms and the market metropolis of Mari, older than memory, by Kalhu and Assur, down at last into the golden city of Babylon. Here, at the northern end of a great alluvial plain, the river flows most closely to its sister, the many-branched, sluggish, shallow Euphrates, two great highways of water carved out by gods and travelled by merchants or armies of men as time dictated. Here also met two great roads carved by men and lined by stately temples and roadside shrines. The Achaemenid Royal and the Khorasan Way connect the grandest cities and most far-flung towns with the centre of Mesopotamia, and, at this moment, the centre of the world of man itself. "A place clothed in purple and scarlet, decked with gold and precious stones and pearls," quoted one old traveller, who had trudged three weeks through sand and hot sun to reach the city in time for the annual spring festival. The old man paused to gaze at morning mist rising from the river and the orchards that backed the homes of the wealthy, and over the glittering rooftops of the legendary temple of Marduk. "Babilim," the old man whispered in his ancient Akkadian tongue. "The gateway of God." He was adjoined by his family to "Hurry up grandfather, or we'll miss the last half of the celebration as well as the first." The old man resumed his walk with a slight spring in his step, inhaling the rich mixture of new smells that rose up in the first heat of the day.

After the spring rains, the air was pungent with the smell of barley and figs, the fragrances of sandalwood and tagara, Indian spices and Arabian perfumes mingling with the odor of camel trains. The caravans flowed, like the rivers, past the outlying farms toward the great city beyond.

It was the time of Akitu. The largest and most eagerly anticipated festival of the year. The streets of the fortress town teemed with activity. Traders could show off their wares at stalls that lined the main thoroughfare of the city, commanding a high price from the thousands of visitors who came from miles around to attend the ceremonies and celebrations. Babylon, already renowned throughout all nations for its wealth and prosperity, became a marketplace for all the world during the fourteen days of this festival of the New Year.

The walls and temples of the city rose up from a flat plain beside the river. The bronzed arch of the Ishtar Gate ushered in throngs of pilgrims who jostled their way through already crowded streets, marvelling at the brightly coloured statues and reliefs along the famous Processional Way. All stopped to gawk at the magnificent Hanging Gardens. Vast terraced steppes festooned with towering palm trees and overflowing with lush green vines in the middle of this desert city, fed continually by buckets of water which rose a hundred feet from the stone floor. "The gardens were a gift from the old king, from Nebuchadrezzar, to his queen," a traveller explained to her companion. "To stop her from crying for her mountain homeland." The two stood gaping at rare flowering plants and bowing trees.

"I wonder that King Cyrus has kept it." The woman shook her head.

"Why shouldn't he?" asked her companion. "The Babylonians built it, but the Persians own it now." The two continued to push their way down the central street toward the Esaglia Temple, the seat of the high god, Marduk.

Between the outer walls of the city and the sumptuous homes of the rich spread out along the riverbanks, nestled the neat clay houses and tidy gardens of the Hebrew quarter. During these days when all the city celebrated the return of the growing season, musicians strolled these rabbit warren lanes and sat in tiny courtyards, strumming their instruments and singing songs of longing and of Jerusalem. They did not call it Jerusalem, of course, though no one in the new Persian government was likely to object. They sang of "she" or "the mother," the beloved, the place where hills rose up, breasts to protect and nourish her children. The words trembled with delicate desire. Songs to the Hebrew god, Yahweh, and to the goddess, Asherah; pillars of their people, they were like springtime to the soul. The goddess's hands were full of pomegranates. Old men and women sat in early sunshine, humming along with old tunes, or straining to catch the sense or rhythm of something new. The minstrels collected tales from far-off travels, blending them with local stories and melodies as a woman might mix exotic scents and oil into perfume. "I don't like this new stuff," one elderly woman sniffed loudly. "Why can't they just keep to the old songs?"

"I hear it's all the fashion in Egypt." The old man beside her drummed his stick on the ground in time to the strange, foreign beat.

A young woman, carefully veiled, lifted her skirt and picked her way expertly through the maze of mud patches and puddles that dotted the busy streets of the Hebrew quarter. She stopped to listen to the music, a traditional tune about white rain falling in Jerusalem. The young woman remembered a song she had heard at the palace, about this rain called snow, which fell from the sky like feathers of a dove, and a lady in a faraway land who lifted a wall made out of paper to look into her courtyard and watch snow fall. The girl felt a soft tug inside her. "It's a test of your character, Shahiroz," her teacher at the temple had told her. "Whether beauty causes you to yearn, or completes you."

Someone called out to her above the strains of music.

"Where have you been so early, Shahiroz?"

The young woman simply smiled and waved and continued down the dirty street. "She's been to the temple," a neighbour suggested.

But someone else said, "She doesn't go there anymore, don't you remember? Cyrus doesn't want so many women priests. Not Hebrew ones, at least. He let all the Hebrew girls go. Shahiroz is learning to make tapestries or something now."

"A shame," another sighed. "To have learned all those stories and prayers for nothing." She brightened. "But that means she'll want a husband now.

What a catch for our Isaac. Her father is still a temple priest, after all. I'll go see Lena, the marriage broker, after Akitu is over."

"You should make a special offering," advised her friend. "To both Asherah and Ishtar. You'll need more than Lena's help to convince Shahiroz's mother to let her marry the son of a mere scribe."

A soft wind pushed up from the river. Shahiroz could hear the calls of servant girls, down at the water since first light, dipping their washing into the river, rubbing it hard against the rocks, then tenderly sucking a corner of the garment to test if the soap was out. Children ran in and out among the houses, shouting with excitement, warbling along with the musicians, their mothers imploring them to stay clean, the servants to haul the water, stir the fire, and get breakfast on so they could all go into town and join the celebrations.

Shahiroz pushed through the door of one of the grander houses and heard her mother calling from the back garden. She paused before the household shrine to the god and goddess. "Remember me," she whispered into the air. "Yahweh, Asherah, king and queen of the heaven, remember your daughter," and she headed into the back yard.

Under a spreading fig tree, Shahiroz's mother and aunt sat in cool morning shade. Her mother leaned over a mortar and pestle, instruments made from fine woods imported from Lebanon. Shahiroz smiled. Her mother was never happier than when bent over her concoctions of seeds and plant cuttings, transforming them into potent tinctures and healing oils. The table before her was strewn with caper leaves to make cleansers for wounds and pale, withered citrus blossoms whose faded yellow and pink petals would soon be crushed into laudanum. Now her mother pressed hard, bruising pomegranate bark to coax out a strong astringent. She was arguing amiably with her sister, who sat idle, sucking pits from soft dates, and popping the sweet flesh into her mouth.

"You can say what you like," Shahiroz's aunt said, "but a snake skin applied to the chest at any time other than midnight is a waste of your time and will harm your patient."

"Of course you'd know far more about that than I," Shahiroz's mother replied. "All I'm saying is that as long as the moon is full, you can administer it at midday and it will work as well."

"That's not what our mother taught us," her sister noted. "She always said midnight, or not at all."

"The time of day makes no difference," Shahiroz's

mother insisted. "That's an old wives' tale. What matters is the phase of the moon."

They looked up as Shahiroz appeared, pulling her veil from thick, dark curls.

"The tapestry mistress sent me home. To tell you you're needed at the palace."

Her mother chuckled. "I love the Persians. They're as stupid as the Babylonians. Only the sixth day of the festival and already they've drunk too much wine and eaten too much pig. A twelve-day festival as old as time. Surely they would know by now not to overindulge too soon." She set aside the half-ground bark and began to fill a cloth bag with herbs and ointments from among many small clay pots.

"I like stupid clients," her aunt said thoughtfully. "They pay the best. Fortunately, I never seem to have any other kind." She poked a date into her mouth. "Is the city crowded today, Shahiroz?"

"It took me more than an hour to walk from the palace to the Ishtar Gate."

"Over an hour." Her aunt's eyebrows rose. "I wouldn't do it. I just wouldn't do it. I don't think there was half the crowd in Babylon for Akitu when we were growing up. I said to Daniel this morning, Why not stay home for once? Just stay home and not battle the crowds in the city. But he's a martyr to his work, my husband. Mind you, he gets cross as a peacock if he thinks I'm overdoing it."

"I'm sure you never give him cause for annoyance," Shahiroz's mother said.

Her sister sighed through plump, delicately painted lips. "King Cyrus depends so much on Daniel. Even more than the Babylonian kings did. Daniel says the king won't make a single decision without consulting his counsellors. He's always asking them what this law is about or how that ceremony has always been done. Say what you like about the Persians, they're wise enough to know when they need advice. And the king can spot talent when he sees it." She paused, a blush rising up under her round, rouged cheeks. "Of course, you're talented too, Shahiroz. No one thinks for a moment that you were removed from the temple for want of ability. Everyone thought it would be you chosen to stand beside the king at the parade the day after tomorrow, representing the goddess. With your dark hair and fair skin you would have looked just like Ishtar herself. It would have been the talk of the festival. And the king loves fair women," she sighed again. "Poor man. Daniel says he hasn't complained, but, you know, the Persian priestess has a face like a camel."

Shahiroz's mother gathered up her bundles of

ointments and potions. "It's unreasonable that you have to go back to work today," she said to her daughter. "It's one thing for me; festivals are high seasons for a healer. But I don't see why you shouldn't have a holiday. I suppose the tapestry mistress thinks that because you're Israelite Akitu doesn't matter to you. I don't suppose she knows that this is only the fourth festival you've seen. Most of the Persians haven't bothered to learn anything about our history."

"It's not the working one minds," Shahiroz pointed out. "If I were still serving at the temple, working during Akitu would be cause for a celebration."

"I like the Persians," her aunt mused. "King Cyrus is very popular. They say it takes him an hour to walk a mile on any given day because he's always stopping to praise every little household deity. I never saw such a king for being appreciative and attentive. He sent his own healers to me to teach them how to make our medicines and ointments. They came every morning for nine days, following me around my garden, asking questions, marvelling at how we grow such plants in the middle of a desert. A scribe came, too, and wrote down every word I said. Daniel was so pleased. I've never been so made up to in my whole life."

"They're stealing our secrets," Shahiroz's mother said. "Then they'll replace us with men. Cyrus is a fool for such a smart man. Men don't make good doctors. They think knowing is better than listening. If the goddess wanted men to be doctors, she would have made them women."

"All I know is that I get invited to just as many feasts at the palace as I used to," Shahiroz's aunt said, "and the Persians make just as good dinners and their women dress even better. They still keep Daniel as a counsellor and your husband as a high priest. And, our food and housing allowance hasn't changed one bit. We were used to the Babylonians because we grew up with them, but I like the Persians just as well, if not better. They treat us even less like a conquered, exiled people than the Babylonians did. Why, Cyrus told Daniel the other day that he has great plans for the Israelite community and that they will likely be sending a good deal of money our way very soon. You wait and see, he's going to restore our shrines to Yahweh and Asherah. Then quite likely he'll appoint the most talented of our Hebrew priestesses to give the prayers to the goddess, and who would be chosen but Shahiroz? He's already rebuilt the shrines to Marduk which the last king let fall almost to pieces. Ah, I see a new fig on that branch. Shahiroz," she observed, glancing up, "shake the tree and see if you can get it down. I like first figs best. The bikurah are always the sweetest." A fat green pod dropped onto the table and Shahiroz's aunt smacked her lips with pleasure.

Shahiroz's mother pulled tight the strings on her bags of medicines.

"Come up with me to the palace," she suggested. "You can help the Persians you're so fond of get over their stomach aches. The king may have his own doctors, but there'll be work enough for us both among the wives."

"We'll all go in for the parade," her sister answered. "That will be enough festival for me."

Shahiroz and her mother made their way through the busy streets of the Hebrew settlement, toward the Ishtar Gate.

"By the waters of Babylon, we sat down and wept and wept for thee, Zion." Music floated through the hot morning air, the voices of old men and women joining in, their longing audible.

"Sat down and wept," Shahiroz's mother scoffed. "Wept to see three good meals a day, maybe. Wept to see our children educated in the finest schools, our men and women given positions of the highest authority in the palace and temple. Our people have never been so well off as we are in Babylon." She breathed in the air, sweetened with Arabian spices. "We live in the most privileged place on earth, Shahiroz. The most magnificent city in all history, I think. The centre of learning, trade and, of course, the very seat of the gods themselves. They say that when Cyrus arrived with his army two years ago, when they came up our great Processional Way, past our fountains and statues, the hundred temples and the palace of the old king, he commanded the troops not to pillage or damage a thing. Declared he had never seen any place so beautiful. And he's been everywhere in the world, I expect. These old people longing for Jerusalem have forgotten what an insignificant little backwater it was. Think they recall a place where the streets were strewn with rose petals."

"But in Jerusalem, we were free," Shahiroz said. "My father says it's our duty to long to return."

"My old mother told me all about that freedom. First, there was the freedom to let ourselves be overrun on a regular basis by every other nation in existence. My mother said they should have rewritten the calendar in Jerusalem: 'Fall festival, winter solstice, first harvest, first invasion: by armies from the north, second harvest, second invasion: armies from the south…' The people of Jerusalem think it's because we're so important, but just look at where the city is placed. Anyone on their way to conquer anyone else is going to march right through, If you're going to lie down in the middle of a busy road, you have to expect to be run over."

Shahiroz suggested, "What about the freedom to prosper from our own work and trade?"

"Ah yes, during those rare periods when we were not actually under someone else's control. Our kings made such continual 'friendship' pacts with other powers, hoping for their protection, that we were usually in danger of being taxed to starvation, or besieged by whatever nation we'd aligned ourselves against."

"The freedom to worship as we choose?"

"People are always free to worship as they choose. So long as they choose what's favoured by the priests and priestesses in charge."

Her mother shielded her eyes, surveying the walls of the city rising massive before them.

"We may thank the goddess to be prisoners here, Shahiroz. Wherever you live you must pander to someone. It might as well be in the most affluent, cultured metropolis in the world, where our boys may learn mathematics, history and understand the movements of the stars themselves, where your uncle is counsellor to the ruler and your father a priest. And where my only child will someday be high priestess in the Esaglia Temple. Babylon has been our home for sixty years. The people we left behind in Jerusalem have forgotten us. It's time we forgot them as well and started celebrating our luck at being the world's most fortunate captives."

The great stone edifice of the Ishtar Gate towered above them. Midmorning sun glistened from the bronze archway ornamented with huge reliefs of bulls, emblems of the goddess and horned dragons, symbols of her consort, Marduk. Here, minstrels played ancient songs, hymns composed before the great god Marduk was born.

The women pushed past a group of religious pilgrims laying offerings of lilies and pomegranates at the foot of a statue of the goddess, hands outstretched to bless her children, set into a large alcove in the inside wall. Worshippers rocked on their heels, faces tilted toward the heavens, murmuring prayers.

"Join them, Shahiroz," her mother whispered. "Most of these poor people will never get within a spear throw of the temple, let alone be able to pray with a priestess. The king's wives can wait a little longer for their tonic."

Shahiroz moved to stand beside the statue. She reached up her hands toward the sun.

"Praise be to Ishtar, our mother in heaven. Hallowed be her name," she called in a clear voice.

Faces in the crowd lit up.

"Who is the one true goddess?" Shahiroz shouted.

"Ishtar," they cried. "Her name be blessed forever."

"What names is she known by?"

"Innana, Isis, Asherah, Ashtoreh."

"What is her dominion?"

"Birth, death, rebirth."

"What are her attributes?"

"Wisdom, justice, mercy, truth."

"How is she known to us?"

"As mother," the people cried, "As grandmother, sister, lover, as shepherdess, giver of life, bringer forth of abundance, as springs of water, as she who nourishes the land, she who tends the fire."

Shahiroz proclaimed, "Let the name of Ishtar be praised by all generations. May she help us to walk in the way of her truth. May she give us bread to eat and minds free to understand her will. May she absolve us of our sins as we forgive the sins of others for her sake. And may hers be the honour, the power, the glory. Let her name be blessed forever and ever."

"Forever and ever."

Shahiroz began to sing. "Who does make the green herb spring up? Mistress of mankind. Who has created everything? Who does guide aright all creatures?"

Voices joined in. "Mother Ishtar whose power no god can approach."

When the last note died away, a crush of grateful well-wishers swarmed around Shahiroz.

"I'm fifty-five years old. I've never said the prayers with a real priestess. Our town is too small to have a temple."

"Do you know the prayers in Persian? We hoped that now that we own the city, my old mother might get to hear it spoken in our language."

"What about Egyptian?"

"Greek?"

"Do you know them in Hebrew?"

Shahiroz moved gently away, smiling. "My mother and I have to go into the city," she said.

"Of course, of course." Many heads nodded. "So much for a priestess to do during Akitu."

An old woman plucked at Shahiroz's mother's sleeve. "You must be so proud," she lisped through half-rotted teeth. "She's regal. Just like the goddess."

"Do you think I should have told them?" Shahiroz asked as they moved away, down the main street toward the palace.

"Tell them what?" her mother answered. "If Cyrus hadn't ended our hope for the first Hebrew high priestesses of the Esaglia Temple, and without so much as word of explanation, I would be seeing my daughter preside over the prayers of the goddess this Akitu, besides joining him in the sacred marriage. Look at the pleasure you gave these people. They'll go home and tell their friends that they prayed with a priestess of Ishtar."

"What if Cyrus never sends me back to the temple? You should teach me to be a healer. As long as there's sickness, people will need a healer."

"And as long as there's a goddess, people will need a priestess!"

"The mistress of the tapestry room says that women shouldn't be allowed to serve in the temple. The Persian priests are saying it's only Marduk who should be worshipped, not the goddess. They say his is the only truth."

"Truth is whatever people believe at the moment."

"If I were healing, I'd be out among the plants and flowers all day, and I'd be doing some good. It's hard to feel the presence of the goddess in the tapestry room."

"There may be no women healers, Shahiroz. Men never feel they have enough power, unless they're king. And even the king is always plotting whom else he might depose. Men without power will try to take the little they think women possess. Why train my daughter into a profession with no future when I can see her standing beside the King Cyrus?"

They passed through the inner ramparts of the city, making their way along the grand Processional Way, a sweeping thoroughfare connecting the Ishtar Gate at the north end of Babylon with the temple of Marduk in the city centre and those of his attendant gods beyond. Here, it was hard to recall that outside the walls, the quiet Euphrates meandered through peaceful orchards and open meadows, and the silence of the vast desert hung in the air. On each side of this wide stone avenue, vendors from the farthest corners of the earth shouted, offering silk shawls from China, soft as spring rain, Persian bath salts delicately scented with jasmine oil, and dark spicy sticks of incense from the flower gardens of India. Shahiroz and her mother pushed past the clutches of travellers jostling each other to get near enough to the stalls to touch hairnets fragile as spider webs or vie for a sniff of rare perfume.

"Akitu is more crowded every year," Shahiroz's mother commented above the din. "Or perhaps it strikes me so because we went so many years without."

The crowd thinned slightly where they left the

section of the Processional Way granted to vendors and began walking past a pantheon of shrines and altars set into alcoves, dedicated to lesser known deities and long forgotten gods. Here and there a small bunch of flowers or offering of nuts or fruit had been placed on the shelf below the icon, and a group of eager travel-soiled devotees huddled close, moaning prayers and petitions in languages the women did not know. Next came E-mah, the temple of the old mother goddess, Ninmah. Its towers shimmered and the walls glistened. Freshly polished relief's of the purple and blue lacquered manes of lions alight in the sunshine.

"The rites of Akitu used to be held here rather than at the temple of Marduk," Shahiroz's mother noted. "Until it was decided that the grandest festival of the year must be presided over by a male god. Men and their need to command. But my sister is right. Cyrus has done a great deal for Babylon. When King Nabonidus left the city, our temples fell into terrible disrepair. Old King Nebuchadrezzar must have been raging in the afterlife, seeing what had happened to his masterpieces. Ten years with no king to approve funds for the shrines. No head of government, no one to keep the priests and priestesses from nearly cutting each other's throats, fighting over which faction was in authority. Most people thought it was the end of the glory of Babylon."

"They say that King Nabonidus was removed from the city because he had a brain fever," Shahiroz said. "His advisors didn't want the people to see his madness."

"Or that he needed time and space to plan some great military campaign," her mother continued. "I've heard all the stories. Why he chose to plot the movements of his army from a distance, in the Oasis of Taima where not a single officer is stationed, is, of course, a mystery they never cared to explain. I've also heard that the Arabian whores are so enticing the king simply couldn't bear to leave. Or, that he was angry with the temple priests who would not agree to worship the god Sin alone, the one called "the light of heaven and earth," the deity whose sole supremacy his mother had championed."

"But worshipping a single god is blasphemy."

"His mother called it a revelation. All proper revelations start as blasphemies, I think. All I know is that King Nabonidus left the city just before the Akitu Festival and refused to return for ten years. So there was no Akitu, of course. Without a king there can be no central rituals. No ceremonial lashing, no penance before the gods, no ritual marriage of the king and priestess. Your father and the other priests had to deal with a few thousand angry visitors arriving here each spring for a festival to find Babylon only a little more lively than a tomb. Then, without any explanation this time either, the king suddenly returns and throws the most lavish, extravagant Akitu in history. The following year it's an even bigger celebration. During which the Persians invaded, taking the city without so much as a fist being raised against them. By next morning, Nabonidus was dead. The priests, of course, announced that it was because he had challenged their authority and offended the god Marduk, although they never did say why it took the god twelve years to administer justice to the king. But then, they see an eclipse and they think it's all about them. Men are like that, Shahiroz. Cyrus has done a great deal of good here in Babylon. And he's shown continuing albeit somewhat inexplicable kindness to we conquered Hebrews. But, he's no different from the rest. It's all part of his vision for himself. You'll see."

They had come to the bottom of the palace steps. A group of ragged peasants, hired for the festival, knelt on the limestone, vigorously scrubbing the luxurious stone inlays of red breccia shot through with white veins. A few of the king's own guards strode up and down the plaza, joking with travellers and firmly dissuading those who thought of camping on the steps.

"I wish I were back at the temple," Shahiroz sighed. "Sometimes I feel as if King Cyrus had me purposely sent to the most obscure position he could find." She laughed. "Which suggests that the whims of a king are all about me, of course. It's just hard to feel close to the goddess in the tapestry room."

"Work and pray, Shahiroz," her mother said. "Pray and work. That's all we can ever do. Things change and change again."

"I remember a story of the goddess Innana that I learned in the temple," Shahiroz said. "The men try to kill her. She remains dead for three days and three nights. Then the spirit helpers assist her to be reborn."

"That's the way," her mother nodded approvingly. "The goddess will never allow such knowledge as yours to be wasted. If the men need to feel dominant, it will be only for a little while. Balance will return, you'll see. Perhaps even for the healers. King Cyrus will come to his senses before long."

In a large stone room, Shahiroz sat silently beside the tapestry mistress, pulling her needle through a cloth canvas, trying not to betray her lack of skill by wincing in pain each time she jabbed the sharp end into her finger. The sound of revellers enjoying the antics of a troupe of street performers echoed through the palace's vast open hallway, even to the remote corner dedicated to the making and repair of the King's tapestries. Shahiroz concentrated on the work in front of her, an old panel depicting an Egyptian goddess with a face like a dog. One of the King's wives had suddenly decided the piece must be restored and hung immediately to honour the Egyptian royalty who had come as guests of King Cyrus during the festival. Outside, voices rose and fell in ribald songs and laughter.

"Listen to them, Shahiroz," scoffed the tapestry mistress, sliding her needle through a rent in the panel. "You'd think they were attending a cock fight rather than a religious observance."

"There aren't any prayers just now," Shahiroz replied. "The priests were at the river early this morning to preside over the daily washing ceremony. There were great crowds for that. I could hear the chanting as I walked into the city. It was very beautiful."

"You can't mean they still do that here?" The mistress was thunderstruck. "The washing is for the goddess Ishtar, isn't it? Purification of the people before her wedding to the god? I can't believe the people here still practice such superstitions."

"The sacred marriage of the goddess and god is the centre of Akitu."

"It is not a sacred marriage between god and goddess," The mistress said tersely. "The ritual you are referring to illustrates the submission of Ishtar before the god Marduk."

"Here, it is the marriage of the goddess and god," Shahiroz responded. "The priestess calls, awakening the god after his long winter sleep, just as she wakes up the world. Their joy in each other starts again the cycle of growth. A joining of equals in love and desire: There is nothing more sacred."

"It is Marduk alone who commands the seasons," the mistress said. "These Babylonians puff themselves up saying they're the most civilized people on earth, but I am shocked at the archaic beliefs the people here still cling to. Thank goodness King Cyrus hasn't been slow to begin reforms. I only hope he takes it far enough. For a great king, he has an unfortunate tendency to listen to what other people think from time to time."

"The goddess is greatly loved here," Shahiroz said, trying to speak calmly. "As I think she is everywhere. Women come from very far away to do their Honour in the temple."

"To prostitute themselves like common strumpets.

Forgetting the modesty and dignity that is the true province of women."

"To give their bodies, themselves, to the goddess. To affirm that our bodies and our desire are gifts that we may choose to share with another, but that we and the goddess alone may own."

"And you do this by parading yourself in the temple, until some man you've never met feels inclined to take you in return for a silver coin?" The mistress shook her head scornfully. "Even Arabian whores demand more than that."

"You don't understand," Shahiroz said. "A woman's body is the image of the goddess. Our bodies are as soft as they are powerful. And for a woman to give her body to someone other than her husband...of her own will...it is very freeing. I see such peace on the faces of women leaving the temple."

"Even a sow after rutting looks peaceful," scoffed the mistress. "If women are encouraged to think for themselves, there is danger. What our great King Cyrus understands, praise be to Marduk, is that the people of this city are greatly in need of firmer control, and that goes for your women especially. No wonder we could capture this sorry place without so much as one arrow flying, or that the people welcomed us in like heroes."

"It was Akitu, after all," Shahiroz said under her breath. "We were all rather drunk."

"The world is like tapestry stitching, Shahiroz. There is a right way and a wrong way to go. Learn the right way and you create something strong and of lasting value. Anything else is chaos."

"Perhaps I'm unsuited to tapestry making." Shahiroz measured her words carefully. "I find it hard to believe in only one way to do things. When my mother heals, she may use aloe to cure the heat rash of one patient, but she knows that his wife might need to be treated with pine gum. In the same way, I know that some seekers find strength and hope in the worship of Ishtar and others in Inanna. There is an old story our Hebrew mothers tell, about a man who could not feel a soul within him, so he decided to take a wife, reasoning that if he owned her he would own her soul as well. But the woman he chose was the goddess, Asherah, disguised. She set the man thirteen impossible tasks before he could marry her: to find a pure white pomegranate, to count the stars in the heavens, that kind of thing."

"And did he complete them?"

"He tried. He spent seven years wandering through orchards and sleeping beneath the desert sky. At last he realized he had come to know his own soul, so he no longer wished to own someone else's. When I guide people in prayer to the goddess, or tell her stories, I try to share a feeling of being safe and loved by her presence. So they may find a pathway to their own soul. Come to know her in their own way. Such prayers have more power than any of the medicines my mother or my aunt can administer."

"Women going about as healers is another practice that will be halted shortly," the tapestry mistress snapped. "Should I ever be asked to marry, I will certainly consider it my duty to leave my post here at once and confine myself to supervising my servants, improving my estate, and keeping myself lovely. King Cyrus will put a stop to such tales as you tell of foreign goddesses. With them will go the misunderstandings of men and women. He is bringing all of our attention and focus to the one true path. Leading us in the way of truth and order. May his name be greatly blessed and may he live forever and ever."

They worked silently.

After a while, the mistress asked, "Why do you have a Persian name? The other Hebrew girls have proper Hebrew names. When they first sent you to me I had no idea you were a slave."

Shahiroz willed herself to reply civilly. "It is our tradition to name children for an ancestor. My mother wanted to call me after her grandmother, Aviv. It means "spring" in Hebrew. But my father couldn't stand my grandmother. She was always telling him how unworthy he was to marry my mother, who was very young and pretty. He was much older and somewhat plain. He told my mother she could choose any other name she wanted. So she chose Shahiroz, which is "spring" in Persian and there wasn't anything he could say about it."

The tapestry mistress let out a short dry laugh. "Your mother sounds humorous. I never think of the Hebrews as having a sense of humour. I mean, what do you have to laugh about? You're little more than chattel here in Babylon."

Shahiroz stifled a cry from a pinprick. She hoped the goddess would see fit to send a suitor to her mistress very soon.

By the ninth day, the day of the grand parade, the streets of Babylon were barely passable. Farming families from the great estates along the rivers now joined the throngs of pilgrims still pouring into the congested streets and overflowing courtyards. Hundreds camped just outside the gates. No one slept. Everyone feasted or prayed, many finding the means to do both. Shahiroz could hear laughter and caroling well into the night. Long before dawn, those outside the walls doused their fires and hurried to claim a good spot just outside the Ishtar Gate, where they would see the Royal Procession come out of the city and make its way down toward the river. A few joined the crowds surging through the archway, down the Processional Way, in hope of securing a viewing place inside the walls.

Outside the Esaglia Temple, the more religious spent the night sharing loaves of bread, barley beer and goddess cakes, small sweet rounds of soft flour and sugar fashioned in the shape of breasts. Some had not moved more than a few yards from this spot since the third day of Akitu. They stood gaping at the steady stream of couriers carrying milk-fed rams, wild boar, ducks, baskets heaped high with ostrich eggs and wine for the palace and temple, or bowing low as the high priests emerged at dawn, walking in slow parade down the Processional Way, out to the river to wash three times and say the prayers of purification required before the ritual marriage. The crowd sang songs to the goddess and to Marduk, joyfully anticipating the ceremony today. Ishtar would call her lover to her side and the growing season would begin once again.

Just after first light, Shahiroz and her mother and aunt picked their way through the throng, walking slowly toward the temple.

"Watch your step, Shahiroz," her aunt cautioned. "The camels have been here. I can't imagine why people aren't made to leave them outside the walls."

The women stopped at stalls offering savoury meat skewers, lamb chunks wrapped in date leaves, and rich decadent yogurt drinks, so precious and perishable in the hot spring air. Shahiroz's aunt treated them to goddess cakes, golden brown, sprinkled with coarse costly sugar.

"Just like our mother used to make," Shahiroz's aunt cried. "Of course now most folk just buy them."

They paused to laugh over a street performance by an ancient Indian whose talent was causing his naked penis to wrap around a stick, before continuing on. A vast array of beauty products was spread out under canopies. "Fine Egyptian kohl," a vendor called to them. "Made only from charcoal of the Juniper plant. The line it draws is so fine and dark, you'll be mistaken for the queen of Egypt or the goddess Isis herself. It makes all other women look like they're wearing soot." Shahiroz's aunt eagerly bought a stash of kohl and a cunning bag, trimmed with feathers and tassels, to hold it.

The women turned their attention to pots of vermilion, a mixture of seaweed, poederos root and red ochre, for rouging the cheeks, and cakes of stark white lead-based paint which gave the appearance of an ivory complexion. "The sooner this goes out of fashion the better," Shahiroz's mother frowned. "I've nursed enough women through skin sickness from using it. Two even died."

"You have to suffer a little to be beautiful," her sister replied, laying down coins for a large tub.

Oils to perfume the hair, pumice stones to smooth feet and elbows. Shahiroz's mother was seduced into buying a small delicately scented, outrageously priced ball of soft wax, infused with fish oil, crushed cyprus berries and new milk, which, when rubbed onto the face each evening for six days, was guaranteed to lessen the appearance of small wrinkles. She laughed as she handed over her money. "I've always been your father's much younger wife, Shahiroz. Let's see if this keeps me looking that way. Besides, your father spends enough on that mixture of olive oil and the blood of a black calf which he thinks will cure his baldness."

A river of bodies flowed down through the city streets, past the E-mah, toward the temple of Marduk. Here, itinerate priests sold charms and good-luck medallions, tiny prayer scrolls wrapped in red papyrus, and clay statues of the gods and goddesses.

"Akitu has become just a way to make money." Shahiroz's aunt clucked her tongue.

Neighbours bumped against them. Lena, the marriage broker, stood in the middle of a large group, busily sharing her store of gossip. Shahiroz's mother and aunt listened along with the rest. With Shahiroz no longer at the temple, they were dependent on others for news. Who had been to make a guilt offering? Who was praying for a quieter home? What woman had gone to fulfill her Honour to the goddess?

"You know the widow Mariah? Married five times. They keep dying on her." Lena crowed. "I said I will have to give her a special rate. She's been to the temple five times. Told each new husband that she hadn't done her Honour yet and off she'd go. She's just married the man who took her in the temple the last time, so that's an end to that deception."

"What about Binyamin's wife?" Shahiroz's aunt asked. "Any takers yet?"

"It's very hard on the homely ones." Lena shook her head. "How long can a girl go on sitting in the temple, day after day, I ask you? It was handled more delicately in our day. After a certain time, they just assigned a solider to do the job."

"Some women say they go to do their Honour

when their own husband has become dull," Shahiroz's aunt remarked. "But my Daniel still makes love to me like a newlywed."

"Still no idea what he's doing, eh?" Lena cackled. "Well, we won't let that happen to Shahiroz, will we?" She turned eagerly to the girl. "I have three fine young men already asking about you. Princes, each one of them. As educated as your father, though not from quite as illustrious families, but then, who is in our little town? And not one of them minds that you've learned to pray and tell stories instead of cook and clean!"

"My daughter isn't interested in marriage," Shahiroz's mother smiled. "She will be called back to the temple before long."

"It's not what I hear," Lena replied. "They say Cyrus got rid of the Hebrew priestesses to hide the fact that it was Shahiroz he didn't want in the temple."

Shahiroz and her mother took a sharp breath.

"Thank you, but I'm not looking for a husband," Shahiroz said quietly.

"Think it over," Lena said good-naturedly. "Before a Persian or Babylonian comes wanting you and you don't get a choice."

Shahiroz and her mother and aunt walked slowly on toward the temple.

"Lena said ..." Shahiroz's aunt began.

"Lena is a common gossip and shouldn't be minded," Shahiroz's mother snapped.

"If Cyrus did not think Shahiroz was suited to the temple, surely he would have told Daniel. Or your husband, who is a temple priest, after all."

"Unless they were the ones he was hiding it from," said Shahiroz.

"A marriage broker is always in the market for a new client," her mother answered. "There's a break in the crowd. Let's squeeze through and find a spot near the steps."

The crowd outside the Esaglia Temple was in a festive mood in spite of the crush of bodies and the heavy sun-drenched air, thick with perfumed smoke that poured down out of the temple chimneys from the sacrifices of beasts within.

"King Cyrus ordered even more scent than Nabonidus," someone beside the women confided in an awed voice. "And all the very best; cinnamon, galbnum and pure frankincense. I heard it takes five hundred kilograms of bread every day to feed all of his guests at the palace. And forty sheep and two bulls and a bullock and eight lambs and seventy birds and ducks and four wild boars and any number of ostrich eggs, and dates, figs, raisins, bushels of pistachios and almonds and fifty containers of beer and wine."

"Fifty-four yesterday," Shahiroz's aunt corrected. "My husband is a counsellor. He told me."

The visitor's eyes opened wide. "It would feed my village for a year."

A crash of music on the steps above signalled that the ceremony was at last underway.

"Mankind is deaf and knows nothing." Shahiroz's aunt tapped her toe and sang along.

"What knowledge has anyone at all? He knows not whether he has done a good or a bad deed. Oh why is god so distant? Why do men oppress each other? I like this one," she shouted above the music. "Catchy tune."

The temple priests appeared, robed in the deep lapis blue of the great god. Shahiroz's father stepped forward and called out across the temple courtyard. "Forgive us, father Marduk. Be with us, help us to prosper. Be our light and triumph always over the forces of darkness." The crowd moaned in atonement, rocking back and forth, murmuring prayers of penance and petition. "May Marduk remember our offerings and regard with favour our burnt sacrifices, may he grant our heart's desire." Shahiroz's father held his hands high in blessing. "May he forever fight our battles against evil and give victory to the king."

A cry of assent went up from the people.

"It hardly matters what the priest says anymore," Shahiroz's aunt complained. "People would rather celebrate than listen. Daniel came in to hear the *enuma elish* five days ago, and he said he could barely hear a word after 'When on high, before heaven or the firm ground below had been named.' Seven hours of the creation story and some talked right through it. Foreigners don't know how to behave at a religious ceremony, that's what I say. To talk during..."

"There's the *urigalla* priest," her sister said.

The high priest took his place in the centre of the landing. Behind him, marching slowly, head bowed in submission, came the king himself. The crowd fell silent. Shahiroz's father crossed to stand between them. He ripped the insignia and symbols of kingship from Cyrus's tunic. Cyrus sank to his knees. The urigalla priest stepped up.

"Do you take on yourself the sins of the people?"

The king nodded silently.

"He does. He takes on our sins." A woman in the crowd began to keen loudly.

"Do you acknowledge the reign of Marduk over all creation?"

"Just Marduk? What about our mother Ishtar?" someone whispered.

The *urigalla* priest held the ceremonial lash high above his head.

"Let the blood of the king, the tears of the god on earth, atone for our sins and secure our salvation." The whip came down hard on the shoulders of the king, over and over in thirty strokes.

"Did he cry? The king must cry." An old woman turned blind eyes toward Shahiroz.

"He's crying," Shahiroz said.

The woman pressed Shahiroz's hands warmly. "Praise be to Marduk. Praise and thanksgiving to the goddess. We will live in plenty this year."

The onlookers were overjoyed. They cheered and sang along with the temple choir, swaying as much as the press of the crowd would allow.

"Clap your hands, all peoples. Shout praises with loud songs of joy. For Marduk the Most High is King. Sing Praises, sing praises. Marduk is King of creation! Isthar is Queen of Heaven."

"Look at my Daniel over there with the counsellors," Shahiroz's aunt beamed. "People underestimate how hard it is to stand quietly in a crowd and say nothing. And your husband did well too. So dignified. So controlled. No one would guess how humiliating it is never to be *urigalla*, but to always be second."

Now a phalanx of palace guards emerged from

the great doors of the temple and strode in formation down the steps into the throng. The masses parted, creating a wide passage through the square and out along the Processional Way.

For the next two hours, the people whooped and roared as huge wooden statues of gods, newly lacquered in brilliant gold, yellow and purple, held high above the heads of priests, were carried in parade. Applause burst out as the image of a favoured god passed.

"Look. There is Ninuta, god of the hoe," Shahiroz's aunt called out. "And Negal, god of war. See the soldiers saluting him?"

"I hear the Persians want to call all the gods Marduk now," the blind woman clucked. "Zababa, Marduk of hand-to-hand fight, Nabu, Marduk of accounting. Why should we have only one name?"

"Just good sense," someone asserted. "One name, one god, one temple. One place to purchase your sacrifices, one priesthood to decide how things should be done."

"Too much power in too few hands," came the doleful reply.

"There's Sin," Shahiroz's aunt continued to exclaim as each brightly painted icon was marched past. "Isn't he imposing? They've carved suns and half moons coming out of his head. And Ada, god of rain. Hear the farmers cheer. Gula, goddess of healing. Stand on your toes, sister, so that people can see us waving to her. So they'll know we're her daughters. And here is Enlil, the god of lordship and counsel. Daniel and the other counsellors are bowing. What a show. Who is next? Look sister, a Hebrew god. It's Yahweh. I'm sure that's who it is. In his guise as god of storms. That's a new form, isn't it? The old Yahweh was a desert god who lived in a tent of camel hair. Perhaps it was hard to show that on a statue. Look at that great cloud he's coming out of. Where is Asherah? Is she next?" But the next giant image was Ishtar. "Oh well, perhaps all the goddesses are becoming one now, just like the gods," she mused. "Old King Nadonidus believed this, and Daniel pronounced him insane. King Cyrus seems to believe it too, but Daniel calls him forward-thinking. I'm lucky to have a husband who understands such things. Though I wish he could explain them to me more clearly."

A pair of priests clad in dark tunics came down the steps, each holding aloft a gnarled and twisted icon, followed by a troupe of sixty small boys dressed head to toe in brown. "Namtar, god of fate," Shahiroz's aunt squealed. "And that awful one beside him must be Negal, god of pestilence." Hisses and jeers resounded through the courtyard.

The unwelcome gods were pelted with date pits and rotten acorns.

More favoured images followed until at last came Cyrus himself, now in a resplendent blue robe brightly embroidered with dragons, carrying on his own shoulders the massive gold-plated statue of Marduk. A great cheer erupted.

"King Cyrus does us proud," Shahiroz's aunt glowed. "There hasn't been a king since Nebuchadrezzar who didn't just walk behind and let soldiers carry the god. No one can say that King Cyrus shirks his duty."

Another roar from a group of Hebrew friends standing at the far side of the steps.

"Who is that?" Those nearby strained to catch a glimpse. "Who is that old man?" A gasp of recognition greeted the man's slow climb down the steps, assisted carefully by attendant guards. He hobbled through the crowd, slightly dazed, guided by the gentle officials beside him.

"It's the old king," Shahiroz's aunt cried. "Sister, it's Jehoiakim. The Hebrew king. Cyrus has brought our king out with him."

"I thought Jehoiakim died years ago," Shahiroz's mother wondered.

"He might have," her sister said thoughtfully. "He looks stuffed. Those two soldiers have to hold him up as he walks. Imagine Cyrus bringing King Jehoiakim back into the city to take part in the Akitu parade. Daniel never mentioned it."

"Maybe Daniel didn't know."

"He must have known. Cyrus tells his counsellors everything."

The last to appear on the temple steps was the priestess chosen to represent the goddess in the ritual of the sacred marriage. Colourfully garbed priests and priestesses of Ishtar filled the upper steps, waving sticks of incense and garlands of flowers. A pale young woman approached dressed in a white tunic, lavishly stitched with gold pomegranates and lilies. Her hand grasped a wand carved to resemble a spreading fig tree.

"Truly, Akitu is a time for jests," a man guffawed. "A sheep is dressed up as a goddess."

Shahiroz's aunt gaped. "She's so tiny, you can hardly see her under all that cloth."

"You would have held yourself like a goddess."

"Hush, mother. They're beginning the prayers."

"Mother Ishtar, sister, lover…" the hymn rang out. The people joined in with the priests and priestesses. "Body beautiful, form divine, wisdom and mercy and justice are thine. Her lips are sweet, life is in her mouth, when she appears, all are filled with rejoicing. What could be equal to her greatness, for her decrees are strong, exalted and pure."

"She's quivering," Shahiroz's aunt giggled. "It's like we're praising a rabbit for its might."

"She'll never manage the prayers," Shahiroz's mother predicted. "She's going to keel over and die before she gets to the song and all the crops will fail."

"But Cyrus cried," the blind woman beside them piped up fretfully. "Isn't that enough?"

"Of course," Shahiroz said quickly. "The crops will grow this year just as every year. The goddess won't desert us because someone chose a mousy child to represent her."

The music ended and the little priestess staggered to the centre of the temple steps.

"Who is the one true goddess?" she cheeped.

"What's happening?" the blind woman asked loudly. "Has she started to pray yet?"

Voices responded flatly. "Ishtar, her name be blessed forever."

"What are the names she is known by?" The words came faintly.

"Innana, Isis, Asherah, Ashtoreh," came the lacklustre reply.

"What is her dominion?" The girl barely whispered.

"I can't hear a word she's saying," the old woman complained loudly.

"I'll say it for you," Shahiroz murmured. She followed quietly along. "What are her attributes?

"How is she known to us? Let the name of Ishtar be praised by all generations. May she help us to walk in the way of her truth. May she give us bread to eat and minds free to understand her will. May she absolve our sins as we forgive the sins of others for her sake. And may hers be the honour, the power, the glory. Let her name be blessed forever and ever."

"Forever and ever." The crowd finished in ragged, unenthusiastic chorus.

"Now the priestess will sing the Akitu song," Shahiroz whispered. "Who does make the green herb spring up? Mistress of mankind. Who has created everything? Who does guide aright all creatures? And we answer, Mother Ishtar, whose power no god can approach."

The young woman stood white-faced, staring into the audience.

"She's going to faint," Shahiroz's mother said.

"There's something wrong." Shahiroz stared hard at the priests and priestesses. "Something different is happening."

The girl appeared to shake herself awake. She

crossed the landing, bent down and placed the sceptre of Ishtar at the foot of the nearest priest. "In the name of Ishtar, I proclaim my subservience to Marduk, who has created everything, who guides all creatures, whose power no god can approach." Instantly, the priests and priestesses gathered around the young woman, bearing her quickly down the steps, out of the courtyard, where cheers issued from the crowds lining the Processional Way beyond.

Stunned amazement. Barely a breath in the Esaglia square. A wail. "She did not sing," the blind woman gasped, crumbling to her knees. "She did not sing."

Moans rose through the courtyard. "Mother, our hope, our protector. Forgive us."

"Have mercy on your children, Ishtar, giver of life," the blind woman sobbed.

"She dishonored the goddess. Our Mother Ishtar." A man's voice broke with fury. "She has stolen our offering of praise."

"We must do something." Shahiroz clutched her mother's arm.

"There is nothing to do. Cyrus must have decreed it."

"Honour the goddess."

"Keep these people from trampling someone," screamed her aunt.

Shahiroz pulled her tunic tightly around her and pushed her way through the howling crowd, walking with purposeful steps up the stairs of the temple. She turned, willed herself to stand erect as she had been taught in the temple, serene and stately as the tree of the goddess. "The priestess reminds us," her voice rang out above the din, "the goddess is faithful to her children, even when we do not admit her. She places her healing powers in the flowers and herbs. She turns the great wheel of the year, bringing us the season of planting and the season of repose."

A roar of assent.

"She lives in our pleasure as we give our hearts and bodies to each other. Remember the story of Akitu. In a time when our mother Ishtar went up into the mountains to enjoy solitude and recall wisdom, the god Marduk plotted to rule the world alone. He commanded all men and women to bow before him, to worship his name only and forget the way of the goddess, which was only that they live in harmony with all creation. When Ishtar returned, she was angry to find Marduk abusing his power and denying the balance of life. But Ishtar's love is boundless and she could not depose him. Instead, she banished Marduk to the underworld for a time. When he goes, she shares lamentations with her people. While he rests, she mourns. When she calls him back, the world revives. Rains fall and the parched desert blooms. With their love, life begins anew."

Shahiroz stretched out her arms and sang, "Who does make the green herb spring up?"

"Mistress of mankind." The response was urgent and relieved.

"Who has created everything? Who does guide aright all creatures?"

"Mother Ishtar! Mother Ishtar. Whose power no god can approach."

Shahiroz lifted her face, glorified. It was so easy. New words began to flow. "Where there is spring, I am always with you. I am the rose of the garden, the lily of the valleys. I call to my love and he answers. Be still my people, do not wake my love until he pleases. Then we will go forth into the field. My love shall be a young hart upon the mountains of spices. I will open for my beloved and set a seal upon his heart. The vine will flourish and the pomegranates bud. I will fill the orchards with pleasant fruits."

"Mother Ishtar. Mother Ishtar. Bless us," a pilgrim shrieked from the crowd. Voices keened in ecstasy.

"Where there is spring, I will always be with

you." Shahiroz lowered her arms gently and brought her face to her hands in closing.

Bodies closed in around her. Faces pushed close, clambering for blessings. Shahiroz reached for her mother's arms. And was pulled through the crowd.

That night, Shahiroz's father did not return home.

This was not entirely unprecedented. With three days of the festival remaining, the priests sometimes slept at the temple, rather than journeying back through streets jammed with tourists, only to arrive home in the last few hours of night, exhausted, bloated and expected back at the temple by dawn. Akitu was winding down, but there were duties for the priests and other officials to attend to. He would be back by evening, Shahiroz's mother assured herself. It was the Sabbath after all, and the New Year Sabbath at that.

Shahiroz's aunt arrived in the morning bearing a restoring poultice for her niece. "Ground turtle shell and goat's milk. Apply to the forehead, no later than midday."

"I met Lena in the street," she ventured. "She went down to the river after the ceremony yesterday, to see the king and priestess go off in the royal barge. She said all those freshly lacquered carvings were almost sunk under the water from the weight of all the dignitaries. Cyrus flew new banners the colours of Marduk. And ten boats full of musicians, all playing at once. People followed along the riverbank, tossing bouquets out into the current. The king had his arm around the girl, just like a bridegroom."

"He was holding her up."

"Lena says a white bull was sacrificed at the marriage house this morning, so everything must have gone well. Although Daniel says the king no longer has to join with the priestess. Just spend the night."

"So many new ideas. Cyrus spoils us." They said nothing for a time. "What does Lena say about us?" Shahiroz's mother asked finally.

"She's a common gossip, and we shouldn't mind her. You said so," her sister fidgeted.

Through the morning, women dropped by to lay small fears at Shahiroz's mother's feet.

"My husband didn't come home last night. He's just a scribe. What would keep him at the palace?"

"Neither of my sons has returned. Has anyone heard?"

"I don't understand. He always lets me know when he's detained. What can have happened?"

"They're drunk," Shahiroz's mother answered briskly. "Or too hung over to face us. Or busy. You know men. They're always busy. Even when they're not."

The women laughed, nodding.

"Some say Cyrus is keeping the men because he's angry," a young wife said tremulously. "Because … of what happened at the Esaglia Temple. They say he'll cut off our food allowance."

"Have a few thousand starving Israelites on his hands because a girl prayed," Shahiroz's mother scoffed. "Go home to your children. Prepare for the Sabbath. Make your dinners. Sweep your houses. Let's not look like we frittered our time away worrying foolishly when the men come home for dinner tonight. Take these mint leaves and make some calming tea," she added. "And a little cucumber balm to soothe your heads."

They went away, reassured.

On the following morning, dinners lay cold and uneaten. Candles had burned into stumps without being blessed. Shahiroz's mother was called into the city, but returned to say that she'd been turned away at the door.

"Perhaps the lady got better," her sister said.

"Perhaps she was told not to let me in the house," Shahiroz's mother answered.

Neighbours appeared continuously. "Go home," Shahiroz's mother insisted. "Tomorrow is the final day of festivities. The men will be in our way again soon enough."

Shahiroz waited in the garden with her aunt and mother, now determinedly deaf to the knocks on the door.

"Lena says that Cyrus will remove the men from the palace and temple," Shahiroz's aunt fretted.

"If that was all, they'd be home by now," Shahiroz's mother said.

"Go to the king, Shahiroz," her aunt urged. "He loves fair women. Say you forgot yourself."

"I cannot degrade the goddess."

"Daniel can't work on the farms. He's been a counsellor to kings."

The Hebrew quarter awoke the next morning to the quiet of the Akitu celebrations now wound down. From beyond the small neighbourhood came tired shouts of pilgrims calling to new friends, sharing blessings for a safe journey and a prosperous harvest, as they headed out of the city. Camels brayed under packs grown lighter. A steady stream of travellers and caravans passed through the Ishtar Gate, heading north along the Euphrates.

A message arrived for Shahiroz's mother. Her daughter's services were no longer required in the tapestry room. No offer was made of work elsewhere in the city.

By evening, the knocks on the door had ceased. Shahiroz remained with her mother in the garden, watching her crush aloe leaves for salves.

Shouts from the street.

"At last. Here they are. Here they are. What has happened? Thank the gods you are safe." Shahiroz and her mother rushed to the front door, straining to pick out one face amidst the jostle of men.

"We have good news," Shahiroz heard her father roar. "The god has spoken in the ear of the king. He has moved the heart of Cyrus. We are free. We are free. We are going home."

From the moment the men returned, the hectic activity in the Jewish quarter rivalled even the busiest day of Akitu. Noise was constant now, lasting far into the night. Families packing and planning, cheers for Cyrus, praises to the gods and goddesses shouted from front doors and on street corners. Old men singing memories of a far-off city. They were going home.

A crone, barely upright, dragged her belongings to the middle of the town centre and plunked herself down. "You're not leaving me behind," she shrieked at passersby.

A woman wailed, "My daughter. She married a Babylonian and she will not come with us."

"Hush Zoe," her husband comforted. "The gods have been good to us."

Shahiroz's father was in and out of houses, instructing the men on what provisions to gather, pausing to reassure the grieving, and to join in praise with those overjoyed. "Our prayers have been answered. Sixty years in captivity, but our god has not forgotten us. We will see Jerusalem again at last."

Shahiroz's aunt arrived, weeping. "Your husband says we may not take our servants with us. Who will wash our clothes? Or do my hair?"

"Better wonder how we will carry enough physics for the journey," Shahiroz's mother answered. "The oils won't keep in hot sun."

"Who cares about your medicines? I'm talking of the necessities of life. It's your daughter's fault," her sister whimpered.

"It was inevitable," snapped Shahiroz's mother. "Did you think that money and housing, the best jobs in the temple and palace, would be given to captives forever? The Babylonians scooped up the educated and elite from Jerusalem, brought us here and treated us like guests, so they could send us back to Israel to behave like loyal citizens. That's exactly what Cyrus is doing now. Waving us home, grateful to our good friend the king, so we'll be dutiful servants of Persia when the Egyptians march through Israel."

"Cyrus set us free," her sister repeated morosely. "Who would have thought the king could play us such a trick?"

Shahiroz went into the city with her mother and aunt to buy up fig cakes and dates, nuts and dried apples, barley flour and a miraculous new grain called "rice" which the Persians had brought with them. Anything that could be packed into bags and not rot in the heat. They searched the stalls for healing herbs and flowers, myrtle, used to treat chest pains, and dried willow, which cured yellow disease.

The women found prices had doubled or tripled. "What can I do? It's supply and demand," shrugged the vendors.

"We wouldn't have to pay such prices if Cyrus had given us more than a week to be gone," Shahiroz's aunt fretted.

"You can give your money to merchants here in the city or to the bandits we'll meet in the desert," Shahiroz's mother replied. "At least the salt sellers don't take it at knife point." Her sister handed over her coins with only slightly less bitterness.

"I'm hiding a vile of cinnamon oil at the bottom of my bundles," she announced. "Don't bother alerting your husband. Even he can't tell me that keeping my hair smooth is not a necessity of life."

Someone nearby started in recognition. "Here are onions." An ancient pushed a bag of bulbs into Shahiroz's hands. "The goddess bless you for preserving her ways."

"Mother Ishtar be with you," Shahiroz answered. Her mother drew her quickly away.

The day of departure dawned clear, the air hot and parching before full light. Children, awaken too soon, cried in the arms of their mothers or slumbered on open ground, heads cradled on packs they would soon have to shoulder. Tears of those leaving loved ones behind mingled with continual prayers of praise and thanksgiving, shouts of excitement from eager young men and the downcast cries of the old, too frail to attempt a trek of six months and a thousand miles.

Shahiroz and her mother took a final glance around their tidy walled garden where the spreading limbs of the fig tree lent coolness to the morning heat. "Who will shake down the *bikurah* now?" Shahiroz wondered.

"Some girl with her own lazy aunt," her mother sighed. "It's time to look forward instead of back. But hard not to grieve. Most of us were born in

Babylon. Our memories are here. Did I ever tell you about the morning I first went out on my own as a healer? My mother and I were together in this garden. She was helping me pack up my herbs, choose which ointments I might need. I was so nervous I could hardly hold my hands steady enough to fill the pouches. I kept asking over and over, what if I do something wrong? What if I mistake a symptom or choose the wrong medicine? Finally, my mother snapped at me. 'What makes you so important? Healing isn't something you do to someone else. It's a journey you undertake together. What's in your bag is not so important as what's in your heart.'"

"It reminds me of the story of Ishtar and the peasant pilgrim," said Shahiroz. "A peasant woman comes to Babylon to worship Ishtar in the temple for the first time. The woman arrived late at night, tired and hungry and was delighted to find small cakes laid out before the statue of the goddess. Surely, Mother Ishtar had provided sustenance for her follower. The woman gobbled up three cakes. Then, bursting with desire to show her appreciation, she determined that, exhausted though she was, she would walk barefoot around the temple seven times, offering prayers of thanksgiving. The woman pulled off her dusty aged sandals, placed them before the statue and went outside to praise and sing. In a little while, a priestess came into the temple. The votaress was outraged to find that someone had eaten the sacred cakes presented as a tribute to Ishtar and, in an almost unimaginable offence, left their dirty cracked sandals near the statue. She stooped down to grab the shoes and toss them away when suddenly a voice from the statue boomed, 'Put those back. The true value of any gesture is whether it comes from a glad and grateful heart.'"

Shahiroz's mother chuckled, "It's a silly tale."

"But it reminds us that, whatever we undertake, the important thing is to approach it with a loving and thankful spirit."

"I wish I could feel thankful about returning to Jerusalem," her mother sighed. "It just feels, somehow, as if we're leaving behind more than just a wondrous city and the place where we grew up. Something of far greater worth than just a comfortable life."

"Things are changing here. It's good to go back to our own people. To the old ways."

"Things change everywhere."

"This is a good change. Father says Cyrus has given us money. We will rebuild the temple. We will worship the goddess in Jerusalem."

"Praise be to the goddess." Rejoicing was heard

in the street. "And to the god. Hallowed be his name. Who delivers us from captivity. Who turns his merciful face to us. Who leads us in the path of righteousness for his name sake."

"May she guide our steps. And bring us safely home."

Shahiroz and her mother lifted their bundles and went out to join the press of people waiting with anxious impatience to begin the journey home.

II
2007 AD

Down the corridor of Hosanna College plodded Professor Reggie Niefeild, arms heavy with books, pondering The Question. Splashes of sunlight pooled in the hallway. Snowdrops were blossoming in the school quadrangle. Crocuses budded in all but the deepest recesses of winter shadow. Outside, the air had grown suddenly warm. Students hurrying through the courtyard balancing books and cell phones and cups of take-out coffee paused abruptly, sniffing the fragrant wind, sensing that something had changed since they buried their heads into books at midterm. The students turned their faces upward, feeling a promise of summer. But, they were late for class or must finish a paper or explain to a professor why they had not finished a paper. They put their heads down and resolutely headed into stone buildings once more.

In Hosanna College, Professor Niefeild reached the end of the corridor and tapped softly on the door of Lucy Brent, his wife and colleague. He waited, heard papers shuffled, drawers open and close and, finally, Lucy's quiet, "Please enter," a little thoughtful, a little dreamy, as if she had been deep in contemplation, rather than reading *Bridget Jones's Diary*.

Professor Niefeild cracked the door and leaned his head inside. "Are you coming for lunch?"

"Oh, it's you," Lucy said a little flatly. "I thought it was Peter. I'm having lunch with Peter."

Reggie nodded. "I thought you might be."

"It's unfortunate," Lucy continued. "But you know, something will have to be done about it. All these people coming to my launch on Friday. Everyone so keyed up. So excited about my little book."

"The first authoritative understanding of the depiction of the Holy Virgin in Pre-Renaissance art," Reggie said promptly. "An important step forward in Marian scholarship. A remarkable achievement in a first book."

"Yes." Lucy wondered if she could coach Reggie to not sound quite so rehearsed. "So much anticipated by everyone. And now this." She offered a faint smile. "Of course, we all know what it's like to have our theories disputed. The to and fro of intellectual exchange. So stimulating. And part of the rigour of academic life after all. So necessary in work of any real importance. But in this case," she sighed with great forbearance, "a little founded on jealousy, perhaps. It's sad to think that in this day and age there are still those who feel threatened by scholastic advancement. By the revelation of truth. They simply must attack." Reggie clucked his tongue sympathetically. He had, in fact, written six successful books on his own chosen topic with never a whisper of challenge from any side, but ten years of marriage to Lucy had taught him that revelation of this particular truth would not be considered helpful.

"You and Peter will sort it out," said Reggie. "Peter knows how to handle this kind of thing. I mean he ought to, after the hoopla Professor Grantum caused last year. Delivering that paper at the Born Again America conference, saying that Saint Paul wasn't so much divinely inspired as bi-polar."

"Professor Grantum was wrong."

"Oh. Yes. That would be a difference between his work and yours, of course. Well, you and Peter will sort it out. I'll come by later and find out how it went."

"What will you do for lunch?"

Reggie was pulled up. "I'll go over to Ned's and get a sandwich. Think I'll bring it back and eat in the lounge. Everyone will be eating in today. We'll all be waiting to hear what you and Peter decide should be done about this."

"So much is riding on my little book," Lucy said once more. "The future of the college. The reputation of the entire university, really. This venerable temple of learning."

Reggie nodded, feeling once again that truth would simply be unwelcome.

A voice boomed beside him. "Am I interrupting a marital discussion or a department meeting?"

Reggie produced the requisite chuckle. "We were just finished. Have a good lunch. Find a way out of this, Peter."

"No such thing necessary," Peter assured him. "The thing is to clarify. Clarify. If the Fine Art department is challenging Lucy's conclusions, then clearly they've misunderstood."

Lucy lowered her head in gentle acquiescence. The Madonna Before The Archangel.

Reggie nodded again. Peter Miller was as good as college principals came, even if his little kingdom had fallen on bleak times of late. Lucy's book, set to come out Friday, was meant to change all that. The college would have two bright stars in the skies of religious academia, after many years depending on the light from Reggie's alone.

"Well, have a good lunch," Reggie repeated. He made his way back along the dimly lit hallway. He had not shown Lucy the two books he'd brought with him. Well, perhaps not the moment for that. Likely, Lucy was not in the mood to consider two new translations of *Song of Songs*, one stunningly transposed into Hindustani and the other into some kind of hip hop lingo. Peter would sort all this out, he assured himself. And, after all, whatever portrait of seraphic detachment Lucy might attempt to present to the world, she could be a lioness in the colosseum of academia. Those in the Fine Art department who had dared challenge her, would find Hosanna's professor of sacred art not going down without a fight. Particularly on the one topic that engaged her mind almost as entirely as The Question consumed Reggie's.

Reggie thought back some ten years to their honeymoon, and, in particular, one sweltering Florentine afternoon spent wandering the Uffizi Gallery. Lucy brushed past the luscious, overripe curves of Titian and Botticelli, then pulled up, staring at the flat, passionless eyes of countless Madonnas peering down from the paintings of Cimabue and Duccio.

"They've captured it, haven't they?" Lucy murmured, with a rapture the artists themselves had eschewed. "Restrained. Dignified. They've captured her."

And now this.

Well, Lucy could take care of herself. Right now, she was probably smiling placidly over her quiche, insisting with gentle concern, "It's just that their critique isn't scholarly, you know? I wouldn't mind what they said if the scholarship was there, but it's not." Reggie felt he could comfortably turn his mind once more to contemplation of The Question.

But the quiche would be cold, the salad too steeped in oil by the time lunch was over. Lucy couldn't eat when she was frightened.

The door of Ned's café was propped open with someone's Latin grammar book. Spring air drifted into the narrow basement cafeteria. A student navigating between the tables to a single open chair forgot for a moment that he had two essays due tomorrow, which could not possibly be finished without a major overhaul of the space time continuum. By the time he reached the chair, the heavier inside smells closed in. His mind returned to being grateful that the university libraries were now open all night.

Reggie ambled into Ned's, oblivious to the spring air. The Question settled into its familiar place, front and centre in his mind. He took his place in line. A student smiled a greeting and Reggie nodded back, assuming that she was in his class in a previous term, or perhaps even in this one.

The line moved slowly. Reggie rested in thought. A cafeteria worker asked him again what he wanted and Reggie surfaced long enough to request a tuna sandwich and salad. He forgot to order a drink.

He walked back across the courtyard, past a statue of a female Christ, arms outstretched, head hanging, largely unnoticed by the steady stream of students and professors. Through the back doors and up the aging steps of the college to the faculty lounge, an airless room, recently updated, replacing the commodious Regency red leather sofa and overstuffed smoking club chairs with beige fabric and straight backs, making the room so properly nonpartisan that most of the staff preferred to eat in their offices. Today, they met in force to discuss the news.

"Forgot your drink again, eh?" Professor Doyle called from the other end of the table. "Bad luck for Lucy this morning. All set to launch her new book, the culmination of all those years of work and the Fine Art department comes out and says her theories are basically bunk. What a blow. But, she'll recover. Many academicians do, I believe. The less important universities are full of them." Lucy was not a great favorite among the other faculty, there being a lingering notion that matters of theological truth were still most safely left in the hands of men.

Professor Doyle read from Lucy's press release. "Coming in advance of what passed for sacred art in the Renaissance, but was in actual fact simply a pandering to weak, fleshy desires among the ignorant masses in which the Virgin is more often depicted as whore than saint, the Pre-Renaissance thankfully provides a vision of contained grace and mild subservience. Here is the Mother, pure and serene in her womanhood. And what did the head of the Fine Art department call Lucy's stark, subdued little Madonnas? Ah yes, 'just bad art.'"

"It'll discredit the college," Professor Laws piped up. "The media will be all over it."

"The press couldn't care less," drawled Professor Cullen. "Look out these windows, gentlemen. Learned men and women all over this vast campus are dazzling the world with theories of merging universes, or laying their finger on the pulse of DNA testing. And we're fretting over sacred art."

"Science!" snorted Professor Doyle. "The secular god."

"A new, improved god. Solves all the troubles we used to lay before the Divine. Cures sickness. Makes us dominant in war. Brings luxury and ease. And all without that inconvenient caveat of our having to behave well and deserve it. Plus, it's solved the age-old problem of hypocrisy that's been such a bugaboo for the church. A new scientific discovery is hailed as having only been possible because of all the right and wrong thinking that went before it. Any truly new religious idea, however, is heretical. We're nailed to our traditional beliefs like bodies on a cross, no matter how senseless, outdated or downright cruel they may be."

"So Cullen, I take it your paper was turned down again?" Doyle said dryly.

"'Ruth: Virtue or Valour' has been accepted, if you must know. A lot of good it will do me. Or anyone. Years of my life spent panning through Biblical texts to determine if the woman Ruth is 'virtuous,' merely an adherent to the chastity norms of her time, as the translators have insisted, or 'valourous,' meaning possessing an inordinate courage, usually only attributed to men, as the original Hebrew suggests. For what? These aren't the stories that tell us who we are now. No one is banging down our doors pleading with us to share insight with the world and demanding we headline *Letterman*. We're a talented group here in the religious bastion of Hosanna, we're managing to publish *and* perish."

"I would like to go on *Letterman*," ventured Professor Laws. "I could explain my theory of Trinitarian conjointment."

"You'd have to understand it yourself first," said Professor Doyle. "You can hardly use public interest to determine what matters, Cullen. Look at *The Da Vinci Code*. Sex. Titillation. Religion as entertainment. It's just giving the people what they want."

"Yes, that's bad," said Laws.

"We're here to provide what they need. Work that will have a more lasting impression on the world."

"An Oprah book selection."

"A return to solid accredited Biblical interpretation."

"Oh, yes," said Laws.

"I believe the end is near, gentlemen," Cullen continued. "Even if our collective reputation is heightened, for the moment, by Lucy's book being a hit. How many have you written, Reggie? All well-received in the upper echelons of academia and none of them enough to keep student attendance from sliding lower than a priest's chance of chaperoning a Boy Scout overnight."

"It's The Question that matters, of course," Reggie shook himself into consciousness.

"The only question is what our lot will do when

God is finally dead and there are no more stories of him left to tell," Cullen replied.

"I might move to private industry," mused Laws. "As a Trinitarian scholar, I'd be snapped up in a minute."

Lunch finished, Reggie plodded back to his office, a room as familiar to him as his thoughts. Books piled high on several small tables, forming towers on the floor. There were more stacked in precarious pyramids on the computer table and printer. Reggie stepped through the maze of volumes, gained the chair and sat staring thoughtfully out the window, soul-deep in The Question.

Reggie wandered in peaceful solitude, musing over one tiny mystifying gem of Biblical wisdom. Three scant pages of ancient text that had engaged his mind and heart for as long as he could now recall. Its setting more real than the world around him.

Song of Songs. Often called *Song of Solomon*.

Amidst the Bible's stories of a small, obscure tribe of people, struggling for survival alongside their solitary male god, a love poem. Setting out the longing of a young woman for her mate. And suddenly, the harsh desert tamed by Abraham and trudged by Moses is awash in spring rain, exotic spices and the lush yearnings of one body for another.

"Primeval porn," Lucy called it. But for Reggie, it was a source of wonder. A love poem. Written by a woman, with nary a mention of god. What was it doing in the Bible? The Question consumed him. Who wrote it? And, why was it placed there? Slipped between the authoritative books of Ecclesiastes, which does not love women, and Isaiah, which loves them less? Why had stern early church fathers allowed it to remain in this most reverenced book? The same men who deemed the mild writings of Thomas and Mary too sensational to endorse.

After authoring six books on the subject, the final answer was still beyond reach. Reggie's mind continued to ramble down well-worn, rather dusty paths.

A sound of knocking came to him from far away, like the tapping of chisel against a stone tablet on some remote Middle Eastern mountain-top, or a Druid carving a sacred sign into an oak. The tapping continued, gradually expressing itself as something from the world around him, requiring response. Reggie turned to the door.

There she stood.

Tall, upright, a mass of black hair falling across her eyes, in a tee-shirt extolling the reader to "Dip me in honey and throw me to the lesbians," and a pair of baggy cargo pants. It occurred to Reggie that students in his classes did not dress as they used to. Gone were the days of smart sweaters and neat trousers. This new style seemed loosely defined as "whatever I could find lying on my dorm floor this morning that doesn't yet smell." But it was not the clothes he noticed so much as the new air of defiant poverty. There was the suggestion that a university degree was a four-year preparation course for unemployment, that the life of the mind, hours spent brooding over Byron or painstakingly parsing Latin verbs, were profitable only to those who issued student loans. Cullen had once declared that this generation's coffee was served by the best-educated barristas in history.

The young woman held out a hand covered in many chunky plastic rings. "Professor Niefeild? I'm Rosie Banks. I'm really, really early. Our appointment isn't until three. But the bus got in early, and I figured I'd just come and see if you could see me sooner. Because, I am so excited to meet you and see the college and talk about what we're going to be working on this summer, and I cannot believe that I'm going to spend five whole months here and study with you and, I mean, you've actually been on panels with Judith Plaskow and Sallie McFague and I am just so, so psyched that you picked me to be your assistant this summer, and work on the new book and spend the whole summer with you just immersing ourselves in *Song of Songs*, just orgasming over the amazingness of it, you know? I mean, anticipation, egalitarian desire. Body beautiful, form divine. Nature veneration, for Christ's sake. Poetic fulfillment. The heart's cry for rebirth. Not all this bump and grind and women in cuffs stuff, though, don't get me wrong I'm so OK with that if it's a safe party and everyone knows the stop word. But like, this is the real shit. We are totally living Joanna Manning's *Magdalene Moment*. Maybe even reclaiming lesbian sex. I mean, goddess, how does the one thing on earth that should belong entirely to women become some kind of power/possession thing for men? It's so whacked, you know?"

Reggie struggled to find something in his experience that would help him make sense of anything this young woman had just said.

"Is it better if I come back later? Our appointment isn't until three. The bus got in early, like I said, so I thought I'd just come up right away and say that I am so excited about being your assistant and I have a lot of ideas that I think will help kind of turn it in a different direction because in your last book, well, in all your books, you say that you still aren't really sure what *Song of Songs* is doing in the

Bible and I really have some thoughts about that. So, I just came up right away."

Reggie managed to move his hand, motioning the young woman to sit. She shrugged off a backpack, knocking over a small hill of books.

"Oh my god, you've got *The Concubine's Song*. I can't believe they let the author of this own a word processor let alone teach at a major university. King Solomon had concubines. *Song of Songs* or, as this throwback to the enlightened male of the Neanderthal era still insists on calling it, *Song of Solomon*, is at least partially written by a woman. Therefore, the book must have been written by a concubine. That's about as progressive as that guy who said that the ancient goddess Catal Huyuk must have had a male consort because, really, how could there possibly exist a goddess without a corresponding god and so, who might this *superior* being be? Why do they hang on to these ideas when they must know they're shit? Oh god, I said shit again. I was going to be so careful when I first met you. Try to make a good impression. You know, like by saying desire instead of randy. Goddam it."

Reggie attempted to slough off the sensation that he'd been shot out of a canon. One moment, left alone to contemplate The Question, the next, confronted by this dark-haired young woman, dressed appropriately for living in a cardboard box under a railway crossing, announcing herself as his new assistant. He did not wish to be called from the foot trails of his mind to where a young woman with fluffy black hair and an alarming vocabulary sat looking at him expectantly.

"I'm sorry," Reggie managed at last. "Who did you say you are?"

"Rosie. Rosie Banks."

" ... you're my summer assistant?"

"We talked on the phone. Three times. You sent me a letter saying I was hired for five months. Is there a problem with this? Because if there's a problem, I've got all my stuff with me ..."

Reggie recalled reviewing resumes of prospective summer assistants. He recalled having coffee with an excellent young scholar from Korea who had asked earnestly, "How do we make the *Song of Solomon* holy? That must be our task. To make it holy." Surely Reggie had hired him. But no, he remembered now that the young man had decamped to Professor Doyle's New Testament department, where he would have no trouble making the epistles of Saint Paul as holy as he chose.

"You're Rosalind Banks," Reggie shouted suddenly. "You're the young woman who wrote the paper on the *Odes of Solomon*."

The head of black hair nodded. "Yes. Can you believe those didn't make it into the Bible? The transgendered imagery of god is just so useful. I mean, who's closer to the yin/yang totality of the divine than a tranie?"

"Thought-provoking work," Reggie beamed, delighted to be on firm ground once more. "My colleagues over at Saint Augustine must have been apoplectic. So, you're interested in working on *Song of Songs*, are you? My new book will consider hypotheses of the church as the woman speaking and Christ as the lover she calls to, the eternal aspiring of people of faith to live in closer obedience to..."

"I want to work on the *Song of Songs*. But, I'm not interested in The Question," the young woman said.

"We must not be discouraged," Reggie assured her. "The Question will be solved. Uncovering the nature of god is meant to be a challenge, a struggle. But I am convinced that the key to this particular mystery is near. A little more thought ..."

"I don't want to work on The Question, because I know the answer."

Professor Reggie Niefeild looked at her blankly. "You ..."

"I know the answer. Why *Song of Songs* is in the Bible."

"Well … of course, conflicting theories posit …"

"I know the answer," she repeated. "Let me tell you."

The young woman began to speak.

In the echoing hall, Lucy pushed at her spinach salad.

"It's just very difficult, Peter. When what my book is trying to accomplish is to clarify so many points of doctrine that people have been anxious about. It's more of a calling than an academic undertaking. I don't see what right the Fine Art department has to judge a calling."

"But we have to speak to this, Lucy," Peter said. "A lot is riding on this book getting profiled. For you, for the college …"

"For god," Lucy murmured.

"Yes, yes, for god," Peter allowed.

"Because, of course, this attack by the Fine Art department is not really about my theories of the depiction of the Madonna in Pre-Renaissance art."

"It's not?"

"Peter, you know it's not. It's an attack on goodness. On truth, and our freedom to express it. And while I would be the last to suggest that the Fine Art department has been hijacked by radical feminist lesbians …"

"It has?"

"That's not what I'm saying," Lucy smiled. "But it's possible that they are, perhaps, just a little knee-jerk in their thinking. A little too bra-burning, if you will. You have to feel sorry for them, missing what's truly at issue here."

"What's that?"

"The eternal struggle. Truth and goodness versus ignorance and evil. My scholarship attempts to guide people back to a place of peace of right thinking. The Fine Art department doesn't understand, so they lash out. I think that's the only way it can be explained."

Peter chewed on his roll. There was no doubt that an offensive of some kind must be devised. Lucy's book was the college's best hope at the moment. Professor Doyle's latest tome, eight hundred pages on the life of Calvin, had sunk like a stone, selling barely a hundred copies, and not even one to the Calvin Institute, who had proclaimed it "uninteresting." Reggie's books drew acclaim, guaranteeing a few more student bottoms in seats and grant monies from the university, but Reggie's next was not due for a year at least. In the meantime, Lucy's book and Lucy's scholarship must be rescued.

Peter could see some merit in Lucy's assessment of the crisis. The classic struggle between good (in this case, Hosanna College) and evil (the Fine Art department of the greater university). Everyone knew the sides. It played to the strengths of the theological mind, offering what was both entirely and obviously clear and rational and yet, remarkably, difficult to understand. Granted, what was good or evil was somewhat a matter of personal taste, but few of the general public grasped this, or wanted to grasp it, and certainly it was not in the best interests of the sensation-seeking media to suggest it.

Of course, the whole thing hinged on Hosanna College's willingness to refer to its own university's Fine Art department as evil. Peter couldn't recall any memos to the effect, but he was pretty sure "Don't declare Satan at work in your colleagues' departments" was one of those unspoken rules of academic etiquette. He could not in good conscience say the Fine Art department was "evil," exactly. Perhaps just "not on the same side as god."

Peter's face lit up. They would announce, regrettably, that the Fine Art department was "not on the same side as god." The Fine Art department would instantly issue a diatribe on Puritanical perversions of sex, conservative churches across the country would produce a zealous, well-funded outcry, the eternal "What is art?" would be bandied about in local papers and an artist opening his first small show on the breast, done entirely in acrylics and cotton batting, would find his obscure gallery picketed and, in deference to public decency, shut down. The Fine Art department would be demonized, but the religious right would be left feeling they'd had a good day out, the artist would be profiled in *People* and Lucy's flat, two dimensional and fully clothed portraits of the Virgin would be hailed as a safe enclave from the unseemly wanton sexuality worming its way into the holiness of true religion.

Peter leaned comfortably in his chair. Lucy picked at her quiche. He smiled. Brilliant woman. The star of Hosanna College in ascent.

Reggie Niefeild sat staring, white-faced, at the bookshelf before him.

After some time, Lucy drifted into his office, slid into a chair, and reviewed the details of her lunch with Peter and how she was quite sure he had "got it." The Fine Art department would be brought to understand, possibly by the press which would denounce them as agents of immorality. The bottom line: Lucy's book would be safe. They could all get back to what mattered: quality religious scholarship. And watching Lucy's reputation soar, of course.

Lucy adjusted her pose, allowing the afternoon light to tint her cheeks like a Giorgione portrait. The Madonna at the Enunciation. She glanced toward her husband. He looked a little odd. Something different about him, though she couldn't quite make out what. A pallor to the skin. Lucy observed Reggie for a moment, thinking it was appropriate for him to say, "Well, that's great, Luce. I knew you'd sort it out. You always manage everything beautifully."

Perhaps she should ask "Are you still breathing?" She watched his chest for a moment, then reasoned that if he weren't breathing, he'd hardly be sitting upright after all.

"Well, there you have it," she said brightly. "Now I must go. Whatever great things are afoot in the Valhalla of academia, the students of Middle World still expect their afternoon lecture."

No response. Reggie was supposed to say, "You're a martyr to your work," with an air of genuine admiration. Instead, he continued to stare, moon-faced.

Lucy was annoyed. Staring off as if one's mind were on higher things was hers, after all. Reggie's was more of a bemused, brow-furrowed, fallen-down-the-rabbit-hole sort of look.

"Well … I must be going," she said.

Reggie continued to stare.

Later, Peter Miller popped his head in, announcing cheerily. "It's all fixed up for Lucy. I've run it past our press secretary. She suggests, "Fine Art Department Doubts God," for the release."

He paused. Was Reggie looking a little odd? Hard to tell in an academic institution. More than once, Peter had been called to deal with professors who paused, frozen, chalk poised before the blackboard, suddenly lost in a train of thought that had little to do with the forty students sitting before them, anxiously hoping that this was the lecture in which something would be said that they could use on the final exam.

Reggie was pondering, no doubt.

"Well, don't work too hard," Peter said. "Stop and smell the flowers. You know. Well … must be …" Peter heaved himself out of the chair and went into the hallway, shutting the door carefully behind him.

By four o'clock, Reggie's office was in shade. He stood up and closed the window. He looked at the row of books on his shelves. Six substantial texts were placed proudly in the centre, each bearing his name. *Sing A New Song: An Exegesis on Song of Solomon*, by Reginald Niefeild, MTS. *Wind and Song: The Holy Spirit in Song of Solomon*, Reginald Niefeild, PhD. *No Greater Love: Song of Songs in*

Historical Context. Song of Songs: Erotic Imagery for Pious Devotion. His favorite, most recent work, *Song of Songs: Lessons from the Q Scriptures.*

Reggie pulled the last book down, looking at his name on the cover for a moment, then carefully replaced it on the shelf. Hesitating, he reached again, lifted down all six weighty volumes, turned and dropped them one by one into his trash can.

Reggie pulled his jacket from the hook, exited the office without locking it and strode down the corridor, out the big wooden front doors, into the softening light of evening. He stopped where the pathway met the main sidewalk, then walked purposefully in a direction that did not lead to home.

Professor Reggie Niefeild headed down University Avenue with no definite plan in mind, except simply to act. His life's work, his very way of being in the world had been negated in a few short sentences by a young woman with fluffy black hair. The unfairness of the situation did not concern him. He had cut his academic eye teeth on unfairness. If life were arranged fairly there would be no need for Biblical scholars at all. The powers that be would have provided one clear, concise set of instructions concerning the plan of the world and our proper place in it. Instead, the most pressing of all questions, such as "What's it all about?" and "What endures?" even, "What the heck did we do to deserve this?" were those least likely to have any answer at all, resulting in the ultimate unfairness; the practice of religion, designed to draw all of humankind together, becomes the most powerful force known to tear it apart.

It was the very unfairness of life that had ensured Reggie a life's work. With no possible chance of an answer, the future was always bright, or, at least, assured. Of course, the unfairness in this particular case was this: a comprehensible, definitive answer had suddenly been given.

So, he flung himself out the front doors of Hosanna College and down University Avenue, not railing against the unfairness of the world, but simply and suddenly feeling the need to act. Now that thinking was done, now that the life of the mind had betrayed him. He needed to act.

Reggie strode past the hospitals that lined the wide expansive street and past several Starbucks, finally heaving himself down on a concrete island in the middle of late afternoon traffic, aware that suddenly acting, after years of making only the most minor exertion, was exhausting.

Gradually, as he regained some breath, Reggie

began to look about him. The concrete island was flanked by midtown rush hour congestion. Behind him, a large and indeterminate piece of public art, a figure designed with as much elaborate detail as a stick of gum, two great arms reaching toward a bird suspended over its head. Hard to tell whether the fellow attempted to catch the bird or to let it go. Below this, purple and white tulips were closing their petals against the evening air.

Reggie sat with his back to the stone monolith, watching the traffic, trying not to think. It occurred to him that there were now new questions to be asked. Questions connected to acting rather than pondering. Questions such as, How will I get warm? and, What will I eat?

"Just go home," was not an answer that suggested itself. His home had been his mind, and he was now exiled from it.

He shivered, possibly for the first time in years. He felt a strange sensation and he found himself wondering what it was. The lines of traffic thinned. Lights appeared overhead. How to keep warm and what to eat became questions needing to be answered soon. He staggered to his feet. Which direction seemed most promising?

"Either way seems fine."

He headed past Chinese food restaurants, the

fragrance of savoury dumplings wafting through doorways. Hot thick aromas and warm lights were not for him, he knew, but for those who had not left their wallets in a book bag beneath their desk. He made his way across Queen Street, through dwindling crowds of those who knew where they were going and were anxious to get there. That Lucy might worry was not a thought that entered his head. Nor did it occur to him to reflect on why it did not enter it.

The street opened into a tiny park, here and there a few ancient trees and scattered picnic tables. Behind the park, a massive stone cathedral, a fortress of religious observance, built in the days when no fortress had been needed. He slumped onto the stone steps of the church wondering, should he sit long enough, if answers to his new, most pressing questions might occur. He huddled close to the wall. Perhaps if he stayed here he might simply drift off to sleep. He wondered briefly about the unfairness of a world where the comfort of slumber was so often made unobtainable by the lack of comfort necessary to induce it. He reminded himself dolefully of where pondering had got him in the past, and returned to the hope that the pain in his backside would shortly become a more bearable numbness.

A half-eaten tuna sandwich was shoved into his hand.

Reggie bit into it, gratefully.

"You coming in?" a voice asked. "If you are, you h-have to line up. At the side of the church. If you don't line up, you know what h-happens."

Reggie gazed up at his benefactor.

"They won't let you in. Once I wasn't there and they wouldn't let me in. Not all night."

The man motioned to Reggie, who stood up stiffly and allowed himself to be led around to the side of the building. A group of men and women milled about in a vague semblance of a line.

"What are we doing here?" asked Reggie.

"Waiting … waiting."

"Waiting for what?"

"Death or god," came an answer.

"Waiting till my girl sends me bus money home," said another.

"Waiting for the goddamned hockey strike to finish," growled a third.

Reggie was enough aware of the world to say, "I thought they settled the lock out years ago."

"They did," said the owner of the tuna sandwich. "Poor Andrew never got over it. A year without h-hockey. It did something to h-his brain, you know? Now me, I didn't miss it," the man continued, "Not my sport. I'm a h-horses man myself. Used to keep trotters. I was a stock broker. Till the crash of 2000."

"I don't recall a stock crash in 2000," said Reggie.

"Not the market. Me."

The man edged closer. "I thought about it one day, you know? That's what gets you. If you think about it. Decided I needed something more dependable. So I came h-here."

The door opened. The group marshaled itself into something more closely resembling a line and filed in.

In a small bright basement, tables were laid with platters of bread and salad. Reggie followed his host to two seats in the middle of the room. The tables around them filled quickly, the harsh voices from outside becoming relieved, eager with the prospect of a good meal. A young woman placed a bowl of fragrant soup in front of Reggie. He dipped into it. The man beside him slurped happily. An elderly lady lifted her napkin and dabbed it to her mouth, a perfect precise gesture.

The bread was soft. Chicken nuggets followed, alongside mashed potatoes, corn and peas: Reggie feasted with pleasure. Then coffee, steamy and strong, and a dessert its servers laughingly called, "Sex In A Pan," a decadent concoction of rich chocolate pudding and sweet whipped cream. Ordinarily, Reggie would have passed on dessert, food being merely something you had to have in order to get through a class or a staff meeting without flagging, but here it was a pleasure, delicious and funny and a reason for gladness.

An old man leaned back after coffee. "You're new here." Reggie nodded. "But I saw you at Saint Anthony's, right? The place with showers? No showers tonight," the man shook his head regretfully. "You got a blanket? They give you one here. Always clean. Smells good. But it's good to have your own, just in case. Last night in, I guess. They close up the sleeping part once the weather gets nice."

"But, it's barely warm outside."

"Well, I'd rather be out than in, anyway," the old man shrugged. "Here come the mats. You want to get moving if you don't want to end up near the door. My arthritis won't take it."

A few men set up camp in an alcove, clearly their domain. The elderly woman found a broom and daintily brushed spotless a small area before arranging her blanket neatly and lying down to sleep. On one side of Reggie, the man with the tuna sandwich mumbled and tossed. The old man slept far from the doorway, silent under a fresh blanket and rumpled sleeping bag. Reggie lay on his mat, under his one clean-smelling blanket. A desk lamp glowed where the night volunteer sat, flipping the pages of a magazine. They would sleep all night with the light on.

Reggie woke too early, the sound of pots clanging in the kitchen behind his head. The scent of bodies. A nagging feeling something was missing. His reasons for living, certainly, this came flooding back to him like the smell of thick, black coffee brewing nearby. Something else. Something else. Reggie tentatively stretched his legs to test their state. Sore. He couldn't recall ever having sore muscles. The new awareness of having muscles claimed his attention entirely.

The man on the mat next to him made a deep snuffling sound, like an animal dreaming. Reggie pushed off his one blanket, his first thought, "Now I must get dressed," followed immediately by "I am already."

Men around him began to wake, issuing gruff morning sounds, stretching their own aching limbs. One or two pushed themselves up, and made their way out to the hallway, scratching openly or patting their hair into place.

The prim elderly lady was awake. She carefully arranged her thin curls. She rose, folding her blanket into a precise, perfect square, placing it carefully at the bottom of her mat.

The old man sat up, talking quietly to himself. The morning activities were fascinating.

Overhead lights were snapped on. A few sleepers still huddled under woollen shields. Most of the men headed out to the bathroom. Reggie followed, returning to find the room emptied of mats, the tables being set for breakfast. A young woman asked brightly, "Can you give us a hand with the tables? I'm sorry to ask. We don't like to impose on the guests. But we have a Girl Guide troupe helping this morning and they can't manage the heavy work." She smiled. "Real jam today. Not that Jell-O stuff."

A clutch of young teenage girls in blue uniforms appeared at the door. The woman headed toward them. "Good morning! Thanks for coming! The kitchen is this way." She herded away the girls.

Reggie worked in silence alongside another man, lifting tables and unfolding their legs. He placed ten chairs at each station. Several people who had not stayed the night ambled in, stamping the cold from their feet.

"My arms hurt," Reggie confided to the old man.

"Oh yeah," he answered. "Don't you worry. It gets better."

"The pain goes away?"

"You get used to it."

"I had that," offered the giver of the tuna sandwich. "You should go to the clinic and see that red h-haired girl. Get something for it. Mind you, if you already h-have the rash too, it's likely too late."

A blue uniformed Guide set a cup of coffee and plate of steaming eggs and toast before Reggie, which made talk of secondary interest. The men applied themselves to breakfast. The scent of hot tea and sausage mingled with the music of clanging pots and pans, the rattling of trays, the chink of knives against jars of real jam, which Reggie found seedy and satisfying and not at all like Jell-O.

"More coffee, sir?" Reggie nodded. The girl carefully tipped the pot to his cup.

"This is my first time here," she offered. "My mom wouldn't let me come last time on account of you being alcoholics. But, I can't get my community service badge if I don't come." Reggie nodded sympathetically. "Mrs. Webb says we should talk to you, because you like that. It makes you feel validated. Why don't you get a job?"

Reggie considered this. "I had a job," he said. "It didn't work out."

"You should get another one," the girl counselled. "They're hiring at McDonald's all the time."

"They won't take you unless you've showered," a man beside them piped up, holding out his cup for a refill. "And an address. They won't take you if you don't have an address. Not just e-mail, either. A phone too. Though they're not always picky about the phone."

The girl appeared struck by this. "You have to have a place to live before you can get a job, but you can't get a job without a place to live?" A few others around the table looked over with mild interest at a young mind being suddenly confronted.

"It's all against you, you see? The system doesn't work and there's no one bothering to fix it. They should ask me if they want to know. I can tell them how fucked up the system is." The Girl Guide appeared equally struck by this thought. She was called away by an older woman in a bluer uniform, suggesting that coffee was needed at the other tables.

The emptiness of the day suddenly loomed. So far, Reggie's plans had included finding the bathroom and washing up a bit, all of which he had accomplished. He might be called on to help remove the tables, though the ache in his arms was extreme.

"I'll see you around." The old man rose from the table.

"I have nowhere to go," stammered Reggie.

"Well, you're a lucky one, aren't you?"

"You go see about that arm before you get the rash," advised the other man. "See that red h-haired girl. She'll fix you up."

Reggie stood up, as the other men were doing. He could put off worrying about the future for another ten minutes, and perhaps by that time, something else unexpected would occur. He decided he would do that.

The park outside the church was emptier than Reggie expected. Two men loitered amid the trees, coughing over cigarettes, trying to find comfort again after sleep which had ended so abruptly.

The old man was holding forth to a small group on the front steps. Reggie edged over to listen.

"What you want to do," the old man asserted, "is to get right in there. You get right in there and get it. Then get rid of it, fast as possible. That's the only way to win at this game. Just get it and get rid of it. Or run like hell so you don't get caught."

Reggie was enthralled. Drug dealers. He had never known any drug dealers. He hadn't even known any drugs. Once, as an undergrad, someone had given him a joint, which he had smoked alone while watching *The Sound of Music* on television.

He had found the movie hilarious until the very end when it turned terribly tragic. By the time the youngest children were toted over the Swiss Alps, Reggie was weeping with all his heart, pledging to devote his life to the well-being of displaced, musically-gifted Austrians. Then he fell asleep.

Now here he was, some sixteen hours outside of the respectable, law-abiding world of Biblical academia, already confronted with the soft seedy underbelly of life on the streets. Drugs. Prostitution. Nothing had been said about prostitution, at least to this point, but he'd always heard the two were intrinsically linked. In any case, he found a certain interest in these dark dealings. He would probably have to become a drug dealer, now that his career as a university professor was finished.

Of course, there was a strong element of not only the illegal but the immoral about dealing drugs. He considered that the same could be said of teaching erroneous theories to eager students, who had trustingly ponied up both their minds and their money. Immoral, yes. Illegal, no. Reggie wondered why this was and, should peddling false truths ever became a crime, how many years a teacher of religious studies was likely to get. Or say, a minister. Or an investment banker. At least with drugs, he reflected, the buyer knew what they were getting.

Knew what permanent damage might result. Besides which, he'd be providing those he served with a few moments of pleasure, something he was not at all certain could be said for his teaching. All in all, drug dealing might be a step up from his former career.

He was saved from something closely resembling bitterness by the old man who was raising his voice, cautioning. "If they're comin' atcha, that's when you've got to run for all yer worth. Just go, Don't worry about the other guys, you just let them take care of themselves."

The men in the group nodded, then began to disperse. One grumbled, "Too late to make the morning rush now. Could be spending my first bit at Tim's by now." Reggie assumed Tim must be their supplier. The old man began a slow amble back around the side of the church. Reggie followed.

"I couldn't help overhearing." Reggie fell in beside him. "I was wondering if, well, if this might be a line of business that I could get into. Naturally, I have some concerns … reservations …"

"You know anything about it?"

"Just that you have to get in and then get rid of it as fast as possible, and run very quickly if they're chasing you."

"That's the ticket," the old man enthused. "Most of these guys, they hold onto it too long. They just stand there looking at it like they've never seen it before."

"I would not make that mistake," Reggie said with assurance. "But how do you know who wants it?"

"Just give it to whoever's hollering loudest at the time," the old man assured him.

"What about the cops?" He was pleased. Even a day before he would have said "police officers" or "authorities." He might do well at this after all.

"Never a worry there," the old man chuckled. "The ones that get involved mostly just want to watch."

Having no moral ground to stand on himself any longer, Reggie realized he could not complain about laxness among the powers that be.

"The only trouble," said the old man, "is when they start to cheer. Gets distracting."

"The police cheer the dealers?"

"Not the Dealers, the Pirates. We was called the Church of Saint John of the Cross Holy Rollers before but we dropped that. The whole sponsorship thing changed the game. You're a big guy. Can you throw? We need a decent outfielder."

"You play baseball." Reggie struggled to keep up. "There's nothing immoral about baseball."

"I guess not unless you steal a base," the old man chuckled. "This is where we play."

They had reached a stretch of open field that flanked the church's back parking lot. The old man waved toward a patch of scrub grass that seemed more free of pop cans and soiled plastic bags than the area around it. "There's games pretty regular. After Thursday night dinner at the Salvation Army. 'Course over here," he said proudly, "is where I spend my real time."

Reggie looked across at another scrap of land, this one not festooned with coarse grass or littered with debris. Mounds of earth rose from the flat surface of the field, surprisingly black and rich, deeply scented with fresh manure.

"This," the old man proclaimed, "is the garden."

"There's nothing here," said Reggie.

"It's underground. Planted most of it last week, soon as the frost let go. Not all on my own, of course. It's what you call a community garden. We get ten or twenty men out here working on a nice day."

"What for?"

"What for?" The old man sputtered. "For eatin', man! For feedin' yourself come July. That's when the first tomatoes come ripe."

"I've never grown anything. I wouldn't know how."

"Nothing to it," the old man insisted. "You got the dirt here and seeds that come from some store that couldn't sell them, or saved over from last year." He pulled a battered envelope from his shirt pocket and held it open toward Reggie. Tiny black dots against the white paper. "These here will go in now. Then you just wait. A bit a weedin' sometimes. A bit a chasin' kids off who think it's somewhere to throw their trash. But just waitin'. The sun comes. The rain falls. And come July you got tomatoes that taste like summer inside you." He looked at Reggie. "You're a big guy," he repeated. "You could help out here, if you want. If you don't have somewhere else to go."

"I don't," said Reggie. "I lost my job. Or it lost me. It turned out my entire theory was erroneous."

"Oh yeah," the old man clicked his tongue sympathetically. "Lost a job that way myself once. Had the erroneous theory I could not go in for a week and they wouldn't fire me. Best thing for you would be to help out in the garden. Sets you up, somehow. Then maybe in between time you can work that corner over there."

"Work it how?"

"Why, panhandlin', of course."

"You mean, I should just ask people for money?"

"A perfectly respectable occupation," sniffed the

old man. "And it's not takin' money for nothin' neither. 'Cause they get a good feeling for doin' it, those who give, sometimes the only time they feel good all day. We had a Jewish fella used to hang around here, said in his religion, someone you do something for should be thanked for it, 'cause they gave you a chance to do a good deed. A misfit, he called it. I don't stick much with religion, normally. But the way I see it, we're providing a social service. Liftin' the morale of our fellow man. Helpin' them feel they've made the world a better place. 'Cause they feel helpless in the face of today's impersonal society," he recited. "It's better than taking money for erroneous theories, I guess anyway. What you're takin' someone's money for can't ever do them harm. You ask me, panhandlin's the only truly noble profession. That, and sheep farming, of course."

Reggie considered his options.

"So, how do you do it?" he asked.

The old man pulled off his baseball hat and began to instruct.

Whatever Lucy Brent thought she was signing on for when she married Reggie Niefeild, this was not it.

At seven P.M. the previous evening, Lucy was sitting expectantly at the dinner table. By seven twenty she was annoyed. By eight o'clock, she was thinking, "If I've finished all this Chinese food by the time he gets home, it will serve him right." At nine, she wondered what meeting or guest lecture he might be attending that had slipped her memory. Ten-thirty brought the realization that any such gathering would long be over. At eleven-thirty she slammed down the telephone, having been informed by the police that a person wasn't missing until he'd been absent forty-eight hours.

"Try calling his friends," the officer suggested.

"He doesn't have friends. And he never goes anywhere spontaneously. He never goes anywhere."

"Is he under a lot of stress?"

"Yes, he's under stress. He's under the most extreme stress. He's a Biblical scholar."

A pause.

"Well, when did you last see him?"

"This afternoon. He was sitting in his office staring at a bookcase."

"That didn't strike you as odd?"

"Why should it?"

"Why don't you go to sleep, ma'am," the officer offered. "We'll call you if we hear anything. Maybe he just got spring fever."

"You don't know my husband," said Lucy.

She telephoned Peter Miller.

"There's the great mind for you, Lucy. He's lost in thought somewhere. Forgotten all about you." This was not completely comforting.

She got into her side of the bed and pulled up the covers.

One-thirty A.M. found her wide awake, rummaging through Reggie's study, searching for the note he must have left earlier that she'd somehow overlooked. Only the predictable lexicons, rafts of scholarly publications, three forgotten phone bills, then *The Collected Poems of Dorothy Livesay*. Obviously, Reggie had pulled this off some shelf by mistake. Lucy paused, thinking about the stash of Mary Stewart romance novels she kept for nights when she knew she'd be alone.

She rifled through the pile of Biblical texts, suddenly recalling how, on their first date, Reggie had joked that, with his command of ancient Biblical Hebrew, he could call down a plague of locusts at any moment, but he couldn't order a beer in Tel Aviv. He had listened respectfully to her description of her latest paper, a treatise on the careless secularization of sacred art, even suggesting a title, *Madonna On My Coffee Mug*, which Lucy used to great success. They walked home from Ned's, Reggie explaining about the strange, resplendent poem that had captured his interest as a graduate student and had refused to let go, with a passion she hadn't encountered in her studies.

There was no note.

She hurried into school the next morning, deeply resenting that she was required to teach a nine A.M. class "My husband is missing" being all the information she felt capable of imparting.

"Any news?" Professor Doyle passed in the hallway.

Lucy remembered to smile bravely.

"He might have been hit by a bus. May be lying in a gutter somewhere."

"The head of the Fine Art department?"

Peter Miller appeared from his office. "Anything from Reggie?"

"Reggie is missing." Lucy's smile became tighter.

"Oh, bad luck," Doyle replied. "He's probably considering The Question. He knows you're not the type to worry."

"I suppose the book launch will be off," Doyle continued. "You won't want to celebrate with Reggie gone who knows where. I might use this as a chance to introduce my new research, 'Humour in the Sermons of Calvin: The Lighter Side of The Protestant Reformation,' a brief work so far, but ..."

"Very generous," Peter injected. "But Reggie will be back before we know it. Lucy's book will get the send-off we've all anticipated."

She went on, up the wide stone staircase. “He will be home soon,” she repeated. In the meantime, Peter was right. She would concentrate on her upcoming success.

Cullen hailed her. “Marvellous. A momentous day. Who’d have thought Reggie would be the first to kick over the traces of this tomb of religious studies? Go in search of greener pastures. Commandeer reality. Embrace a new world.”

Lucy paused outside her classroom. She set her face, and went in.

With the first shovelful of dirt, Reggie Niefeild knew that he was not cut out to be a gardener. The old man was swinging his spade expertly, bellowing out a meandering song long out of fashion, probably for good reason, all about women, heartache and the effects of cheap wine. Soil cascaded around him into rising piles.

Reggie’s shoulders screamed. In spite of a slight breeze, he was sweating profusely. Another new sensation, like hunger and cold and waking up amidst strangers. Dust sprayed into his eyes and throat. He coughed painfully.

“Is there water?” he asked.

“There’s a fountain over there,” the man gestured. “Sometimes it’s working.”

The water was warm and fusty, but Reggie gulped it gratefully.

By noon, they had dug a sizeable number of rows. Permission was given to haul water from the church tap. "Corn kernels like wet ground," the old man explained, as he and Reggie dragged bucket after bucket across the field.

Reggie removed his soaking shirt, spotting a twenty-dollar bill in the pocket. A fortune. He and the old man headed around the church, over to McDonald's. They feasted on Big Macs and cold pop.

His clothes felt soft and heavy with dust. Smelled of new soil. He held the plastic cup against his cheek, enjoying the cool smoothness. The old man licked the last fatty sauce from his fingers, grinning.

"Now that's what I call a feed. When you're hungry from doing something that matters. I have to say, for a big fella you don't have a lot of muscle. That'll come. When I first started, I didn't have none at all. Hard to think it now, eh?" He displayed a boney forearm. "You have to keep it up during the winter, of course. I go down to the food bank four, five times a week and stack boxes. Good to help those less fortunate." The old man smacked his lips and pushed the tray aside. "Yessir, that's what I call a well-deserved repast. Now we better get going. Time for siesta."

The two men crossed back over the street to where several men lounged at the picnic tables in the afternoon shade. Reggie noticed white blossoms scattered like confetti across the sparse grass. A cool breeze ruffled his untucked shirt. "Do we go back to the garden now?"

"Rest first," the old man answered. "Got to keep with the rhythm of the body. Personally, I favour the top of one of these tables. Don't feel so hard as the ground, somehow. Here, Bill!" He poked at the man who had bestowed the tuna sandwich and who was sitting idly on the nearest table. "Get off of there and let a tired man rest."

The old man motioned to Reggie, who heaved himself onto the table and folded his arms across his chest, convinced, nonetheless, that falling asleep in a busy public park was simply not possible. This theory would also prove erroneous. There was a rhythm, after all, as the old man had said. He drowsily admitted there might be something in this idea, just before he drifted off to sleep.

He woke in the sudden chill of late afternoon, realizing that falling asleep on the top of a picnic table was not nearly as uncomfortable as the after-effect of falling asleep on a picnic table. He sat up stiffly, gently massaging the throbbing muscles in his neck, regretting his failure in the past to lift anything heftier than a Hebrew lexicon.

The old man was no longer stretched at a table nearby. Reggie wandered back around the cathedral to the garden.

The old man was close by the plot of earth newly readied for corn. He was speaking excitedly with two very young, very well-dressed men in nice suits. Reggie had never owned a particularly nice suit, but it was interesting to him to see that one could instantly identify a nice suit when you saw one. Light, lustrous, hanging in folds of substance without weight. He stood still, transfixed by the sight of blue material luffing gently in the breeze.

"Reggie, get over here and help me tell these folks how things are," the old man demanded. Reggie shuffled over, trying hard to concentrate on what was required.

"These men," the old man puffed, "want as how those of us using the community garden should tell some city planning fellas that we don't mind if this land gets given over to development."

"With room for community use, of course," one of the men interjected. "A percentage will be set aside for green space."

"Space the sun don't get to," the old man answered. "So yes, we do mind."

"You see, the thing is," Reggie offered, "As I understand it, the garden project is a necessary, albeit unregulated component of the community health and social system here. Access to nutritional supplementation, as well as self-sufficiency stimulation. A building development wouldn't address either of those issues for this particular demographic. Theologically, the issue might be said to be …"

"It's good for the economy," one of the men cut in, brightly.

"Which is, in fact, a sound theological stance, 'the economy' being something we tend to consider synonymous with, 'the general good' a force to be recognized and served as a typical post-modernist approach to existence and societal roles, but also a valid hypothesis of any orthodox religious path. The issue would be of course, what hermeneutics are you applying to the adage, Good for the economy? Questions which naturally suggest themselves being, *Whose* economy? and, Can, in fact, 'economy' be *different* than what's good for people?"

All three men looked at him blankly.

"I'm sorry," Reggie stammered. "I'm not used to talking about real issues."

"You go on," the old man said. "About the hermits."

"Hermeneutics. It just means how you interpret things. Particularly scripture."

"We're not building a place for a bunch of hermits here," one of the men stated. "Greenway Inc. cannot support groups with a religious affiliation."

"What I'm trying to say," Reggie picked his words over slowly and carefully, "is that we assume that what's good for the economy means what's good for all people. But this may not be the case. It may be good for some, but actually harm others. Those traditionally excluded from participation in economic benefit, for instance. I suppose I would posit that there may, however, be one use that benefits everyone. A garden, for instance."

More blank stares.

"Fresh foods make the men here less of a burden on the health and welfare systems. Green space lowers stress among urban dwellers. Land is more desirable that fronts on a park or ravine, so it's serving the economy of those who own local property."

"We're builders," one of the men piped up. "We're giving people what they need."

Reggie nodded sympathetically. "It's hard when you find out you've done the opposite."

"Tomatoes!" the old man smacked his lips.

"They're what everyone needs. You come here in August and tell me if anything you make is half so good. Big, juicy. Fellas here call 'em Tomato Tits."

The men stood shuffling their feet. Reggie wandered some feet away, staring into the inky soil of the new garden. Soft, fine shoots showed just above the ground where the old man had planted last week. Reggie suddenly wondered if the soreness he felt had anything to do with his new acquaintance with sleeping mats or shovels. Perhaps something he'd layered over with thought, the life of the mind. No amount of rest would speak to this ache.

He slid to his knees, burying his hands in loam warm from the sun. The scent of manure. Life and decay.

A voice at his side. "What do I do? If I find that out? That I've done the opposite?"

He let the dirt flow through his fingers. "You come here," he said.

Reggie's first night outside, his first without a real dinner, was easier than expected. With coins left over from buying lunch, he purchased hot dogs and pop from a street vendor, which he shared with the old man who regaled him with stories of lettuce, crisp like morning air, and strawberries sweet as kisses, which would be theirs in the summer. The old man knew what spots were best for sleeping, protected from night breezes, where one was least likely to be interrupted by security guards or other passersby. He showed Reggie the way to tilt his body so that wind or people were rebuked.

"Couldn't we sleep in the garden?" Reggie asked.

"You'll want to be comfortable," came the answer. The old man led him to a nook at the side of the church and curled into the position he'd suggested. "The garden will be there when you wake up, son," he said sleepily. "It'll be there tomorrow."

He hunched on the ground as the old man directed. Soon, snoring issued from the body beside him. He pulled his jacket closer and shivered. He decided that, since he was not sleeping yet, perhaps he would walk over and see what was happening at the garden.

High lights cast a hazy glow over asphalt and stubble. A group of youths huddled at one end of the field, voices rising in laughter, curses. A police car slowed. He could feel tension arise. The car moved on and the shoulders of the young men relaxed. They slouched off down the street, shouting too loudly for the time of night.

He plodded over to the garden patch, wondering what he expected to see. Still a stretch of dark earth with a few faint wisps of green showing forth. He sat down beside the mound and wondered, if he placed his hand to the ground, could he feel the seeds growing. Under the carefully tilled earth, beans must already be pushing, prodding their way from their soft shells. Cabbages starting to stretch out and sense which direction light came from. Tendrils of peas unwrapping, beginning to sense their strength.

The moon rose over the cathedral church, baptizing the garden in light.

He was still cold, but he felt better sitting here, bathed in soft luster, the warmth from his fingers encouraging new life below. The ache that was not in his body continued, but seemed more bearable now. Something larger than himself grew beneath the place where he placed his hand.

In the morning, Reggie panhandled for their breakfast money, finding it surprisingly easy to ask for coins with the knowledge that, in exchange, he was doing no harm. He worked in the garden alongside the old man, astonished to find that the pain in his arms and legs hardly troubled him once the spasms in his back set in. At lunchtime, Bill came by with sandwiches, not tuna this time, reportedly given by a Salvation Army lunch wagon. The three men sat on a picnic table, munching contentedly.

"You h-hear about the game tonight?" Bill asked. "We could use a big fellow like you."

"What time is it?" Reggie asked, from habit.

"Whenever it starts," Bill shrugged. "After rush hour, of course. Money to be made during rush hour."

"I've never played baseball."

"Nothing to it. All you need is a steady h-hand. Just a steady h-hand." He held up trembling fingers. "I play catcher."

After siesta, Reggie and the old man returned to the garden. They placed sticks to show which seeds had been planted. "Here will be beans," the old man grunted. "Beautiful vines they grow into. Spread all over the place. We'll use more of these sticks to hold them up. We stacked the ones from last year under the steps behind the church, but someone pinched 'em. That's the bugger of owning things. You have to worry all the time."

"Maimonides," murmured Reggie.

"Newminster," corrected the old man. "Best beans going."

"Maimonides was an ancient Jewish philosopher. He envisioned pain as a kind of pyramid. The bottom third, the largest part, is the pain we cause ourselves. With worry, resentment, envy, self-doubt, that kind of thing. The middle third is pain we cause each other." He paused, thinking. "Then the smallest portion, the part at the top, is pain that comes simply from being human. Disease, natural disasters ..."

"Head lice," the old man said sagely.

"Or just the aging of the body."

The man grunted. "So, the most pain in the world is what we can do something about?"

Reggie nodded. "If the world isn't Eden, it's because we don't choose it."

"Sounds right to me," said the old man. "I guess My Moneys was pretty smart. No wonder. What with god being Jewish and all."

Reggie stopped. "God is Jewish?"

"'Course he is," the old man said. "Everybody knows it. His son was, after all."

Reggie felt compelled to say, "Jesus, the divine in human form, was Jewish. That doesn't mean you can attribute human characteristics or ... or affiliations to god."

"What about anger, jealousy, retribution?" the old man countered. "Being mad if women are priests or two men care to marry each other? What about loneliness? Didn't god make Adam for a friend?"

"Well, yes, but ..."

"What about longing?"

"What?"

"Longing," the old man said. "Don't you think god longs for something?" He stopped and surveyed the garden. "What do you think it might be? After all this time?"

Lucy left her afternoon class, returned to her office and sat with hands folded in her lap, trying not to scream. She had spent a second night alone, not sleeping. She had combed through Reggie's papers and texts once more, admitting finally that there was no point searching for her husband among his books. Calls to peripheral friends and their few relatives only increased her distress. No hospital reported an unidentified patient of large stature and with a preoccupied expression.

She sat quietly at her desk, reminding herself that the police would search when it was appropriate to do so. In the meantime she must wait patiently, accepting uncertainty and affliction with serenity and grace.

"Goddamn it!"

She left her office, stalked down the corridor.

Nothing unusual or out of place in Reggie's office. The same high shelves crowded with books, His heavy wooden desk, his chair with a cushion of faded reds and gold, a gift, years ago, from a student visiting the Holy Land. The same casement windows as in her own room, showing the quadrangle from a slightly different angle. The windows had not been opened though the outside air was mild, making it unlikely that anyone had been here very lately. She dropped into Reggie's chair, wondering what she'd hoped for.

Lucy struggled to recall any word of Reggie's, any passing remark or even a look that might have warned her something like this might happen. What *had* happened?

She pulled open the desk drawer. More Dorothy Livesay. If this woman wasn't deceased, Lucy might have been jealous. She flipped it open. "... underneath the hanging/scrotum cluster/red buds bursting..." Practically obscene. This woman called herself a spiritual poet. She should be ashamed. Lucy turned a few pages. "Dreams... like words you keep pushing around... till they fit..." More inscrutable poetry for Reggie to lose his way in. Then, she recalled again that first evening together. He had read to her from his beloved *Song of Songs*. And for a moment, nothing else had mattered in the world. But, that ancient longing. And the answer she saw in him.

She closed the book. Placed it carefully back in the drawer and gently pushed it shut.

She looked up.

A blank space on a shelf. In the centre of the bookcase opposite.

Space. On a shelf.

This simply did not happen. For both Lucy and Reggie, the question was always where they might find more space for books. Their apartment living and dining rooms were overrun with books. Research texts choked their hallway closets. They had removed bedside tables, reasoning that a stack of Biblical commentaries did the job just as well.

A foot and a half, empty. On Reggie's shelf.

Her first thought was, "I could put some of my books there." Followed by, "Reggie would never leave an open space." She glanced around at books piled on the desk, behind the desk, under the desk. The same as ever. Books upended in the small trash can beside the desk. Not the same. Six books. Six solid, hardcover volumes with titles Lucy knew as well as her own name. *Sing A New Song: An Exegesis on Song of Solomon*, *No Greater Love: Song of Songs in Historical Context.* She lifted them up and placed them before her on the desk. She had a sudden chill. Some Master of Divinity student, driven mad by receiving a B- term paper, had murdered Reggie, dumping his life's work into the trash. The foolishness of this hit her immediately.

Reggie's teaching assistant was responsible for grading term papers.

She picked up a volume. *Song of Songs: Lessons from the Q Scriptures.* Reggie's most recent offering. He had said something about it. That it represented something. "Everything he'd longed for." They planned to celebrate its launch with dinner at a restaurant just slightly beyond their means. But Reggie had gone into his study instead of dressing, becoming absorbed in notes for his next book. Lucy had sat down to proofread a paper.

She ran her hand over Reggie's book. She would have her own, come Friday. The thought was wildly exciting. She was sure it was.

Slowly, she picked up the volume before her. The reward of a life wholly dedicated to the sincere and educated pursuit of truth. She raised it above her head. She heaved it with full force at the bookshelf. The binding cracked, pages splattering to the floor.

What right did Reggie have not to feel fulfilled?

She reached for another, sending it crashing against the far wall with a satisfying smack.

Reggie had dropped these books into the trash can. Of this, Lucy was certain.

What right did Reggie have to realize that his work was not enough? And, to say it as clearly as if he'd stood in this room in his rumpled jacket, and his remote expression?

Sing A New Song sailed through the air.

What right to blow off the accolades? The respect of his colleagues? Forbearance of his wife?

No Greater Love exploded in a spray of leaves.

Lucy waved another book high. This thing he had loved above all else.

The hand did not move. The book was placed on the desk. Lucy sat, shaking inwardly.

"It isn't enough," she said.

That evening, Reggie was assigned to left field.

The group of musty, unshaven men sorted themselves into teams, with some efficiency. Timeworn baseball mitts were passed around. A sizeable gallery of locals collected at the edge of the field, passing thermoses of coffee. Reggie accepted a tattered glove and went to stand in the area the old man indicated, struggling to recall what he knew about baseball. He decided that the man presently holding a mottled tennis ball would, likely in the quite near future, throw it toward the man holding the mottled bat who would, in turn, attempt to hit it. This might send the ball sailing through the air, possibly in Reggie's direction, in which case he would step neatly aside and someone else would catch it.

Behind the field, the towering apartment buildings were awash in the orange and red evening light. Reggie shaded his eyes against the glow. A sudden crack. Shouts and scuffling. A teammate at Reggie's right limped over, scooped up a rolling ball, and threw it with some skill toward the folded newspaper that marked first base.

Scattered cheers from the sidelines. Now there were two men standing on first base, so Reggie assumed the ball had not been fast enough. The man beside him smiled and shrugged, limping back into position.

Reggie smiled back. He didn't know why. It felt good to be out in cool evening air, deep scarlet flames warming his tired back. Reggie stretched his arms above his head. It felt good to simply exist and to feel. Reggie reached toward the dying sun. "It will rise again tomorrow," he thought. "The rain will fall and the old man's garden will grow." Something appeared in the air above him. He stretched further. A battered tennis ball dropped into the centre of his glove.

Reggie pulled the ball out, tossing it lightly to the player beside him, who heaved it smartly toward the hat marking second base. The old man called approvingly. The light behind him began to dim softly. Streetlights clicked on, brightening the field.

Sometime later, Reggie looked up into a blackened sky. The playing field was empty. The old man was sitting beside the garden, humming. Reggie sat down beside him on a pile of earth.

"I'm married."

"Oh, yes?"

"She doesn't know where I am."

"She'll be worried?"

"I don't know," Reggie said truthfully. "But it's time I go find her."

A brief nod. The old man staggered to his feet, shambling off toward the church.

Reggie stood up, and crossed the ballpark toward Yonge Street.

"Over here." Under the furthest streetlamp, at the edge of the green, stood Lucy. "I've been calling and calling," she said. "You didn't answer." Lucy held out her hands. "I've come to take you home."

"I have something to show you."

They linked fingers and walked back across the field.

III

By the third week of travel, chatter had ceased. Shahiroz rarely saw her mother, always on call to tend blistered heels, eyes parched by the sun, backs sharp with pain from lifting too-heavy packs. Then the larger cares: women whose babies did not come easily, or who were too weak to walk with an infant strapped to their chest. The group moved before dawn, children drowsy, old folk hobbling alongside exhausted cows and sheep. The men and older boys walked ahead, the women trudging behind. In the afternoon, they rested, then went on for a few more miles, until stars glittered over the black Euphrates. They slept on bare ground, the river singing them to sleep.

Some turned back. They'd sooner take their chances in Babylon. Cyrus had agreed to keep the scribes and accountants; perhaps there would be other opportunities. Some had gone elsewhere from the start. Some headed to Egypt, having relatives there, others to Cunaxa, where there was promise of work. Those walking to Jerusalem, bathing cracked feet or searching for a place to rest that was not wind-slashed or stony, realized that freedom was, at least presently, more pain than privilege.

During the day, the highway brimmed with activity. Vast caravans, one hundred camels long pushed the stream of travellers to the edges of the road. Itinerant farmhands bound for the orchards of Mira passed with waves and songs. Shahiroz walked with the women, encouraging confidence, telling tales to draw the mind away from burning feet and swollen ankles, relaying information obtained from her father.

"We take the same route our ancestors did when they were marched to Babylon," she said. "We will retrace their steps and reclaim our liberty. First, we go north to Mari, there's a market there. Father says we may stop to buy whatever we need. Then, we head west across the desert. It's the narrowest place to cross. We'll walk only at night there."

"Because if we saw it in the daylight, we wouldn't go," muttered an elderly woman.

"Then down a little to Damascus. And just below there is *Yerah Shalom*. Jerusalem. City of Peace."

"*Yerah Salem*," the woman corrected. "City of

Salem. It was named for the ancient god of the evening star. Makes more sense if you ask me. When has Jerusalem ever been a place of peace?"

"Sometimes a name speaks to what is possible, rather than what is. It's a magical city. My father has told me. The sky is dazzling, endless. It cleanses the mind of earthly distractions. It draws the soul upwards, always, toward the heavens and the divine. Our ancestors felt that.

"There is no easy access to the sea there. The ground is too steep and broken in most places to allow the use of carts let alone chariots. The nearest trade routes are miles away. There's little wood for burning, little ground any better than rubble for pastures or planting. It is a city that exists for one reason only. When you are there, you feel the holiness of being alive."

They passed by orchards festooned with scarlet blossoms, smelling of new grapes. Shahiroz pulled up handfuls of flowers, weaving them into garlands, bestowing them on the oldest crones and youngest girls. "Tokens of The Mother," she said.

"What mother forces her children from their home?" an old woman fretted.

"Jerusalem is home," Shahiroz assured her. "Cyrus has given us money to rebuild the temple."

"Cyrus paid us to get out of town."

"In Jerusalem, the goddess will crown us with roses," Shahiroz promised.

The ancient one nosed the bouquet deeply and grinned.

With the first new moon, Shahiroz reminded her father that the women must rest. She gathered the children. "One day, the god of the sun decided that two monarchs could not share a single crown, so he diminished the size of his counterpart, the moon," she told them. "But the moon asked, Are we not equal in the sky? Why then, must I be made to appear smaller? The sun realized that the moon was right, but had no power to change its state. So the sun decreed that once a month, all women must be released from work. They gather together, honouring the light of nighttime with prayers and fellowship. The moon was satisfied."

The children clapped and laughed.

Shahiroz led the women apart. A bonfire glowed near spreading trees.

"New moon, ancient light," she called out. "You are the guardian of women, the sentinel watching over our repose, the power we imbibe as we prepare to begin again. You draw on our bodies and we live with the rhythms of waves. Hear our prayers. May this be a month of blessings for your daughters."

"Of joy," a woman began the petition.

"Strength," suggested another.

"Of dignity," a third voice pleaded.

"Kindness."

"Enough rest."

"Good health," Shahiroz's mother's voice.

"Friendship."

"Courage."

"May the truth and justice of the goddess guide our actions," Shahiroz finished. "May we prosper in this time of spring." The women nestled together, passing a camel skin wine bag, joking riotously, tossing twigs into crackling flames.

The next day, Shahiroz's father called her to walk beside him.

"I'm trying to recall the story of the great flood," he said. "Cyrus would not return the tablets and scrolls our captors stole from the Jerusalem temple. It's hard to distinguish between which tales are our own, and which we learned in Babylon."

"Tales are like my mother's medicines; more potent for the mixing."

"Why do you think we tell stories, Shahiroz?"

"To remind ourselves that we are safe and loved."

"More. They tell us who we are, what our place in the world might be. My father used to say, we don't create the stories of our people, they create us. The story you told last night … do you know why the Babylonians overran Jerusalem, destroying the temple?"

"Our king made a pact with Egypt."

"Yes, and the Babylonians carried off those of us who were the leaders, the scholars and priests. When we return, we will need to reestablish authority. The tale you told last night … a sun wishing for power, a moon refusing to be diminished, it does nothing to help our people understand what is needed now."

"It teaches us to challenge injustice. It sanctions time set aside for us to rejoice together and to recall the renewing energy of the moon to which a woman's womb dances."

"It encourages women to waste time gossiping and swilling like peasant wives at a carnival. Not to recall the grandeur of their role in the task before us. These are remarkable times, Shahiroz. Miraculous, I think. We must cast off the attitude of slaves that we were forced to assume in Babylon and realize the glorious mission we have been called to, the resurrection of the glory of Israel.

The role of priest and priestess has never been more important. There are new messages to teach, ones that will help us to rebuild our nation. We must tell stories that are strong with Yahweh's will that we be welcomed back into Jerusalem. Tales that proclaim the god who champions the children of Israel. Whose desire is that we increase as a nation, the temple its centre, the place where tales are told that teach how we may survive as a people, unified and unending. Teach that in your stories. Celebrate it in your songs and prayers."

"Alongside our other tales, of course."

"You must understand, Shahiroz. We are returning to a broken city and a severed tribe. Reunion, healing, restoration, these can be our only concerns. You have great gifts, Shahiroz. The women trust you. You have a talent for leadership, for inspiring right thought. Use those gifts now, for all your people. And please help me recall this flood story. Then I can tell it in a way that will say something helpful."

"I remember the man was called Utnapishtim," Shahiroz said slowly. "And that, at the end, an ale house woman sings a song that goes. 'Gilgamesh, fill your belly day and night, make merry, let every day be filled with joy. Dance and make music. Gaze at the child that is holding your hand, and let your wife delight in your embrace. Those things alone are the concerns of men.'"

"A cautionary tale of those who thwart the laws of god. We'll call him Noah."

Their first stop on the journey proved disappointing.

"Mari must be Babylonian for 'not really a town,'" was the suggestion.

"Not a single rampart," Shahiroz's aunt wondered.

They camped outside, the women filing in to purchase packets of tasteless spices.

"What can we do?" vendors complained. "The best goes to the city."

The way now turned from the river into the desert, the landscape rocky, parched, unchanging. The sun arched the sky in a blinding glare. Silence hung over grey brown hills, as unrelenting as the heat.

Thorns slashed careless travellers. Shahiroz's mother emptied her cache of aloe and began canvassing among strange desert plants for anything to calm a pain or halt infection. Now and then they would come across swaths of white blossoms sprouted from some secret hold of moisture, or emerald leaves gushing from a rocky crevice. "Capers," Shahiroz's mother cried. "Excellent for healing cuts and scrapes. Thank goddess for your prayers, Shahiroz. Asherah has not forgotten us."

Ash grey trees spiked the endless barrens. The monotony of the landscape and walking enervated the body and depressed the spirit. Shahiroz searched her memory for stories to entertain and encourage. When they paused to rest, she sat among the women offering another from her store of tales, holding a child in her lap, or sometimes standing before them in order to act out the full range of characters being portrayed.

"A man came before Asherah, petitioning the goddess for assistance. 'Oh great mother,' he cried. 'Even though I work from dawn to dusk, still I am poor and cannot feed my family. My house is at the side of a lake. To get to market, I must walk all the way around. Even if I start out in the middle of the night, by the time I get there, the other farmers have taken all the customers.

"'You who are all powerful, all gracious to your children, please teach me to walk across the lake so that I may get to market in time to sell my wares.' Asherah was pleased with the man's sincerity, so she granted his wish and taught him the secret of crossing the water unharmed.

"The next week, the man's neighbours were astounded to see him head off to market, shouldering his pack of goods, walking straight across the lake without sinking. One of the neighbours, a lazy farmer who did little to care for his wife or children, saw the man walk over the water and said, 'Well, if that's all it takes to get to market, I too will go. I'd like a day out.' He stepped into the lake and immediately sank in over his head and was drowned.

"When the first farmer returned that evening, the neighbours crowded around him asking, 'How is it that you could walk on water and this other could not?' The farmer replied simply. 'The goddess did not give me the power to walk over the surface. She showed me where the stones were beneath.'"

The women laughed, forgetting for a moment their aching muscles and exhausted spirits. The children clambered for more, until finally Shahiroz bid them lay on their blankets, singing them to sleep under enormous stars, with words of hope and promise, the return of joy and of spring.

One night, her mother lay down heavily beside her, smiling in spite of her exhaustion. "I think I will cease to worry about finding new salves and ointments, Shahiroz. You do more to heal these people than my little store of medicines can ever do."

They nestled close. "If we reach Jerusalem in time for the autumn festival I can sing the lamentations of the goddess atop the plateau where the temple once stood. My father says there was a massive platform on one side. People used to squeeze in to hear the prayers and songs of the priestesses. They were packed in even more tightly than in the courtyard of the Esaglia. Thousands of worshippers, coming together to mourn the passage of the dying god. And there was a room in the centre of the temple called The Holy of Holies. It was said to be the place where the highest god lived. No one was allowed to enter it. Except for once a year, when the high priest would go in all alone."

"No one else? Who cleaned it?" Her mother scoffed gently.

"I suppose the gods don't care about dust," Shahiroz smiled. "This year, my father will be the high priest."

They lay, gazing upwards.

"The goddess' headdress," Shahiroz breathed. "The stars are gleaming gemstones and the moon, a brilliant jewel set in the centre. The deep black sky is her hair. I wonder if the gods truly care about us building temples. The one they made themselves is so glorious."

Shouts from the men's side of camp. Angry voices punctuated the still air.

"They should be resting," Shahiroz's mother

reproved. "What's so important that they wear themselves out like this?"

"A new temple," Shahiroz said. "One made out of stories."

She snuggled further into her mother's arms and slipped contentedly into sleep.

The longer they walked, the more feverish discussions among the men became. When they moved, when they rested, while women and children lay on hard ground, packs under heads, Shahiroz's father and other elders huddled together debating, recalling, reshaping.

Did Moses make seven miracles or eight? Seven was a sacred number of Marduk. Seven days in the Babylonian's calendar. Eight, then. No, ten. What commandments were most important? Serve our gods only. Survival by numbers. What was that story? The woman who betrayed her people? Married outside her tribe?

What stories to keep?

The saga of Ludlul, the man whose faith the gods tested by taking from him all that he treasured. They'd call him Job.

What words to sanction? The prophets warning of alliances with foreigners. Those who worship other gods.

What to leave out?

The Book of Norea. The men considered this venerable, beloved work, a tale glorifying the first female as the pure, undefiled source of all true wisdom.

"This is not useful," the argument ensued. "And Yahweh is portrayed as arrogant and ignorant. This tale is blasphemous of the god who ensures our safety and survival."

"The work excites women to forget their role," it was added. "Just as stories of the goddess do."

"Yahweh, who decrees our return to Jerusalem, must be reverenced and obeyed."

"Yahweh alone."

"Power cannot be shared without being diminished."

"The women will understand. This is best for the whole."

There were rules for personal behaviour, religious duty. Instructions for building the temple, the priests its heart, ensuring the precise and proper sacrifice of the burnt and the sin offerings. Leading the prayers. Enforcing laws. Interpreting the scriptures.

"What do the men talk about all day?" the women wondered.

"How to secure our position when we reach the old city," Shahiroz answered.

"Our position!" Shahiroz's aunt cried. "Daniel's family owned a thousand acres of land right outside the walls. Our father had more."

"Those left behind have bought the land from the Babylonians."

"They'll be delighted by our return. Who could be happy farming land that's not really their own?"

"What's this the men are saying about women being freed from attending prayers in the new temple?" A young woman shouldering an infant confronted Shahiroz. "My husband can have that freedom. Let him stay home while I go and pray."

"They say the *enuma elish* is heresy. There's a new story of creation," piped up another.

"It's ancient," Shahiroz said. "There's a legend that it was taught to our people by Moses who might have learned it from his wife, because it's a desert story and she was from a wilderness tribe. It goes like this. The first man and woman inhabit an oasis. Groves of date palms, almonds, oranges."

"To live in a garden," a woman murmured.

"But they must not eat of one tree. A serpent appears assuring them, however, that the fruit of this tree will make them wise as gods. The woman eats, the gods are offended, and the two are exiled from the garden."

"Typical. Anytime a woman tries to better herself."

"It teaches that disobedience brings suffering," said Shahiroz.

"Who decides the meaning? The one who tells the story, or the one who hears?"

"Trees and snakes are symbols of the goddess' abundance," someone fretted. "And how does Yahweh make this garden all alone? A birth without a mother?"

"The female is the wind sweeping over the deeps, just as in *enuma elish*."

"This goddess has no name."

Shahiroz went to walk with her father. "I've neglected my duty, being only with the women."

"You're unmarried, Shahiroz," her father frowned. "You may not be here."

"A priestess," the girl stated, "may always be with her people."

"You defy your father?"

"We are equals in matters of the gods. I have been considering what stories of the mother best speak to the worries of our people at the moment. Some of the women are concerned about when they may do their Honour to the goddess. They ask how long it may take to build the new temple. I remind them that the goddess' true sanctuary has no walls. There is the tale of Asherah and the woman who is crippled and who cannot come to the temple. It reminds us that so long as there is sincere intent..."

"Tell the women not to trouble themselves. We are assembling a most wonderful and useful group of stories."

"We will want to include those of the spring awakening, of course, and the lamentations of the fall festival as the god dies once more. Also, those that remind us all that pleasure may be shared, but that our bodies belong to ourselves and our divine alone."

"Our bodies belong to our husband, our wife, our people, Shahiroz. To the increase and continuance of our race."

"My body is not just a tool for increase. When the time is right, I will worship the goddess by fulfilling my Honour. The other women will too, as we have always done."

"You are not hearing what I'm trying to teach you. We must keep ourselves to ourselves. Yahweh commands it for the survival of his children. We are remembering the whole history of our people. We have glorious songs of those who delight in a god who protects us and fearsome tales of those who disobey. Proof that Yahweh intends that we reestablish his temple in Jerusalem. We have the poems of our great King David, rejoicing in the righteousness of Yahweh, calling for his wrath upon any who threaten to diminish us."

"Wonderful, indeed. But David sang to the goddess as well as the god. He bowed his knee to Asherah, as did King Solomon in the temple he built."

"Things are different now, Shahiroz. The old ways do not serve us anymore. Tell the women we may rejoice. We have been granted greater wisdom."

"What greater wisdom exists? What should we rejoice in except our place in the flow of creation? No delight is greater than knowing the divine presence equally in birth, death and rebirth and in all that is male or female, stone or blade of grass. Nothing is more fearsome than forgetting that the only justice is that which ennobles all creatures. When slaves are freed, so are the masters. There are no better stories than these."

"They are not the ones we need to tell."

"They're forever the ones we need to hear."

"We have different troubles now, Shahiroz. We are called to rebuild a nation and rebuild a temple to keep that nation together. Whatever does not serve that purpose does not serve god. We will return to Jerusalem. We will proclaim that which glorifies Yahweh and his plan for us to reclaim the city and re-establish our people. Then the stones themselves will call out with psalms. The rains will sing hallelujahs. We will make a temple, more magnificent than the first. Imbued with finer knowledge. You will have the great joy of knowing that you helped make this possible by ceasing to share stories that mire us in ignorance. I have explained what is required. You must begin to educate the women."

"That in remembering our history, you have forgotten the goddess?"

"By telling them to give praise and thanksgiving. Yahweh has opened our eyes to see more clearly."

Shahiroz returned to the women. The men were worried, she explained calmly. Anxious about how they would be received when they reached the old city. There was nothing to fear. All would be well when they were safely established in the city once more. The demands for assurance that the ways of both god and goddess would be respected, she answered, "Yahweh is a sky god. Lord of thunder, wind and air. The goddess resides in the belly of the earth. You cannot leave out half of creation and expect it to be whole."

From a moonlit crag, they saw a rise of palm trees in the distance. "An oasis!" The cry swept through the line of travellers like desert wind. "Fresh water, fruit. Maybe a few days respite!" A small party went ahead to assure the desert people, who must surely inhabit this paradise, that the horde of sand-caked skeletons was not an army.

"Army!" A lean, toothless desert-dweller howled. "We weren't sure you are even human."

The band returned with reports of a hundred camel hair tents billowing in the night breeze, a host of women and children, herds of goats and sheep and, most important, promise of a hearty welcome.

"They're called Ahl al-ba-ir in Babylon." Shahiroz's aunt shuffled eagerly on chafed feet. "It means Those Who Love Camels."

"People of the Camel," Shahiroz's mother corrected. She joined them to share the merriment. "The animals are precious as date palms. They give milk, skins, dung for fuel, urine for medicine. I must ask about that."

"I hear they eat locusts," a woman tittered nearby. "Roasted and dipped in honey."

"I'd eat sand to have a change from dried date cakes."

The desert men crowded around their guests, gesturing hospitably, insisting their leaders take wine with the head of the tribe. Their wives filtered among the group, smiling at the Hebrew women, asking to hold the babies, offering baskets of plump apricots, melons fragrant and fleshy. Pouches were topped up with cool spring water. Children were treated to handfuls of sweet roasted corn.

The desert women's wrists were ringed with glittering bracelets and henna stars, their hair scented with musk. They unrolled carpets, ornately woven, placing them fireside for the Hebrew women. One wife sought out Shahiroz and her mother, leading them to a place of honour.

"You are wife and daughter of the *shaykh*, yes? My husband is also the chief. He is old now. He dyes his hair with saffron because it is too thin to take henna. I am the youngest wife, so I can do whatever I want. It is very pleasant."

"It's so agreeable here." The Hebrew women bit into soft, fragrant pitas.

"It's just where we stay right now," the woman shrugged. "The camels eat ground date pits, but the sheep will want grass soon."

"Where will you find it?"

"A storm will come. Sprouts will grow in the wadis. The sheep can smell it from half a day away."

"You'll move all of this?"

"What is there? We have what our hands can carry." She inspected Shahiroz. "This is your only daughter? Why is she so old and yet unmarried? There is a wedding in two more days. You will all join us. We will show you magnificent hospitality. You will tell the world of our splendid wealth and manners."

The Hebrew women slept under fleecy quilts. In the morning they scrubbed their children's faces in shady pools. Young men of the tribe gathered to watch the Israelite girls gaily bathing each other's necks and hands. The youths' skin was brown, their limbs sturdy as pillars. Eyes, milky blue. The air was sweet here, fragrant with myrrh and the water intoxicating as new wine. The girls lowered their gaze as cooling liquid trickled over tanned arms.

Shahiroz went with her mother and aunt to seek out the female healers. They found them sitting cross-legged on richly woven carpets under waving palms, chattering over their work. Some were carefully sorting faded leaves and shriveled berries into small piles. Others were mashing what looked like ground palm fronds into a paste along with a thick, honey coloured liquid that smelled strong and sour. One woman was occupied stitching camel skin medicine pouches, intricately embroidered with tiny perfect roses set amid artful olive-coloured leaves. Silver bracelets shimmered and jangled over dark skin as she deftly pulled bright crimson thread through fragrant, supple hides. Shahiroz wondered whether the tapestry mistress would have pronounced these nomad artisans as backward as all other non-Persians. Surely, the exquisite detail of their designs would have forced her to reconsider. Only a refined soul could create something of such intense and delicate beauty.

The women laughed over their work, gaily anticipating the festivities planned for the next day, declaring themselves delighted to share their store of knowledge with the Hebrew women. They waved the guests to shady comfortable spots on the rugs, pushed baskets of dates and apricots in their direction, produced gourds filled with refreshing drinks, urging them to taste a little passion fruit, have a another sip of cooling water and vying with each other to display their wisdom and expertise.

"Newborns must be put into a bath of salt and camel urine each day for one week. It will ward off infection."

"The cure for tight bowels is dried *acadia* leaves, ground to a fine powder and given with camel's milk."

"At what time of day?" Shahiroz's aunt asked.

"The time is not important," the desert women

assured them. "Such ideas are superstitions. What matters is the direction of the wind."

"If a person is possessed by an evil spirit, you must touch a red-hot knife point to the centre of their forehead," offered another. "The spirit will fly out through the skin where the mark is."

"A woman who is barren should listen to pleasing music before lying with her husband."

"Weakness in the head should be treated by cutting off the hair. If that doesn't work, the person must coat their scalp with orange oil."

"And avoid all arguments. Particularly after dinner."

"Where do you find herbs for healing?" Shahiroz's mother wondered.

"No one is more aware of the world around them than our people. We notice every line in the sand, every alteration of the breeze or flicker of a lizard. A good healer can see a green sprout growing from very far away."

"But, do many flourish?"

"Desert plants have roots stronger than the rays of the sun. They may be dormant for a long time, but need only a little water to sprout. A seed that has lain in sand for a hundred years may still germinate with a good rainfall."

The women worked and talked until the sun was

high. Slowly, yawns began to replace advice. Pestles and pouches were laid carefully aside. Hands dropped into laps. Eyelids drooped. A few of the women languidly packed up their work and wandered off toward the tents. Others simply curled up on the carpets and closed their eyes. Shahiroz's mother smiled drowsily and laid her head down. Her aunt stretched out in the pleasant shade. Soon, the noise and bustle of the camp was stilled.

Shahiroz lay beside her mother, watching slivers of sun glitter and dazzle amid the emerald green leaves above. A breeze rustled the palms, brushed delicate patterns in the sand. Then, soft strains of music. Notes from the single string of a *rabab*. She got up quietly and went in search.

She found him sitting beneath a date palm. Upright, sturdy as the tree, his skin bronzed, teeth gleaming. She remembered a song, "His teeth are like white sheep on the hills of Gilead." The young man looked up, fingers suspended over his instrument.

"Don't stop. It's so lovely."

The young man smiled. His eyes were lapis blue. "Like the sky over Babylon after the spring rains."

He began to sing, his voice stirring as the desert breeze.

"From the crimson of your lips, I drink again,
As if I were the thirstiest of travellers that ever
sought water.
Do not deny me, my Euphrates, my Tigris.
Your kisses are sweet as water from the
foothills of Mark-hul, from Hibbara.
None who tasted of their streams was ever so
slaked as I."

"So beautiful," she said. "Are you a poet?"

"All of our men are poets." The young man lowered his *rabab*. "It is considered the highest accomplishment. I have made this to sing at the wedding tomorrow."

"Are all your poems about love?"

"About love, yes, but also about honour, heartache, longing. All are matters of importance to the tribe. Memories of times of trial, scarcity or famine. Tales of our most glorious victories in battle, our most esteemed heroes. These poems have everything: grandeur, a noble moral. Everything. But historical accuracy, of course."

His eyes sparkle when he laughs, she thought. Like sunlight glinting on the Ishtar Gate.

"So, your poets are your priests," she said aloud.

The eyes shone again. "Better than priests, I think. A priest will tell you how to act. A poet, how to live."

This time, Shahiroz laughed too. "Who is being married?"

"My brother. To our cousin, because he cannot marry our sister."

"Surely—"

"There is an old saying, 'The best wife for a man is his sister.' He knows for certain whether the girl's reputation is unblemished. And most importantly, whether he can abide her mother." He paused and grinned. "But, it is not fitting to marry a sister, of course. So, if possible, parents arrange for their sons to marry a cousin. In this way, no wealth is lost to the family and all descendents increase their prestige."

"So, you also will marry a cousin?"

"When the time comes. And you?"

"I am a priestess. I may lie with a man to fulfill my Honour, but I cannot marry."

"What strange wishes your gods have."

"I suppose the ways of other people always seem strange. We're so used to our own we think of them as right, not just habitual. It's good to be reminded that 'this is the way we do it' is not the same as 'we do it because it *is* this way.'"

"Perhaps priestesses may teach how to live as well as poets."

"We are encouraged to reflect on the meaning of things."

"Here, we do not have so much reflection, I think. The rains come. The sprouts grow in the wadis. There is not much else to know."

"Except what to put in love poems."

"But that, no one can teach. We may only learn from what our heart tells us."

Shahiroz's breath quickened. There were small creases around his eyes when he smiled, though he could not be more than seventeen. They were like soft furrows the wind makes in the desert sand. His hands were strong from holding the reins of a camel or a sword in battle. Sensitive enough to now pull from the instrument another strain of silvery, sweet melody.

"Arise,
Come into the garden.
I sleep but my heart is awake:
It is the voice of my beloved that knocks,
Saying, 'Open to me.'"

"I know this," she gasped. "It's an old song. A hymn to the goddess. It was performed at the spring festival long ago, when the rites were held at her temple rather than that of Marduk. There are two parts. One for the priest, one for the priestess. It portrays the goddess calling to the god. Awakening him to new life."

"For us, a man and woman wishing for each other," he answered. "Sing with me."

Shahiroz searched her memory for a moment, and then began.

"I call to my love,
Arise, and come away.
For lo, the winter is past and the rains are gone.
Flowers return to the earth. The time of singing is come.
And the voice of the turtle is heard.
Let him kiss me with the kisses of his mouth:
For his love is better than wine.
My beloved is like a young hart upon the mountains of Be-ther.
His eyes are blue. Like rivers of waters, washed with milk."

She faltered. "I…I'm not sure what comes next."

"Her lover responds. Like this.
She calls the north wind to blow that spice may flow.
Behold, thou art fair, my love;
Behold thou art fair.
Thy lips are a thread of scarlet.
Thy eyes are deep as pools in Hesh-bon, by the gate of Bath-rab-bim.
Sustain me with new wine. Comfort me with apples.

I am sick with love, oh my dove.
Thou as ravished my heart.
You are the rose of Sharon
A lily in the valley."

"With delight I lie in his shadow," she answered softly.

"Our bed is green.
He sets a seal upon my heart,
His banner over me is love."

He finished,

"My beloved is mine and I am hers,
We were intended for each other since before
time was thought of.
Behold the gladness of my heart."

The strong fingers strumming seemed to tremble as the young man picked out the closing notes.

Her dark eyes met his.

"Shahiroz?" Her mother's voice. Tentative. Not far away.

He held out his hand. "Come tomorrow."

She touched the outstretched fingertips. Fire. She nodded. Then hurried away to where her mother was calling her name. Behind her, the melody of a *rabab*. A hymn of joy.

The next morning, the women of the Hebrew camp rose to the sound of wedding preparations underway. Savoury stews of boiled grains, onions and spicy meat simmered over hot coals. A man paraded past, proudly waving aloft the severed heads of goats.

"The bride's father," they were told. "Assuring the tribe of a lavish banquet. You will be in awe at the abundance of the meal."

Shahiroz went to bathe with the younger girls. The girls chased each other through the shallows, splashing joyously, making tiny rain showers with cupped hands. Shahiroz joined in the game, laughing until she could run no more. Later, scrubbed and refreshed, she wandered through the nomad women's area, eagerly sampling grape leaves stuffed with crushed nuts and dates, soaked in honey, joking with the women working, reveling in the excitement of a festival. She drifted happily, licking the last precious dabs of sweetness from her fingers.

On a carpet, brushed scrupulously clean of any grain of sand or fleck of soot, a group of women bent over the folds of a lavish garment, glistening with real gold thread.

"The bride's robe," one of them explained. "These are the finishing touches. She will shine like the sun for her bridegroom."

"What is the wedding ceremony like?" Shahiroz sat down at the edge, carefully keeping her sandals well away from the shimmering dress.

"It is magnificent," the woman assured her. "The groom's father goes to the tent of the bride's. He says, '*Salamm w aleykem*. Peace be with you.' The bride's father answers, '*Aleykum as salamm*. With you, be peace.' The groom's father offers two camels. He leads the girl to his son, who waits at the marriage tent. Then, we feast, and the new couple battles."

Shahiroz was picking a wisp of palm frond off of the carpet. She stopped. "You mean that the bride and groom fight?"

"Of course. A female camel will never mate willingly. We had one that rampaged through the camp. She tore up many tents before they could hold her to the ground and let the male camel complete his coupling. In this same way, should our young women not also be modest? A bride is expected to resist her husband. And, he should try his best to force himself on her. It is true most girls do not choose to fight for very long. But now and then we have a good joke the next morning, over a groom's blackened eye or broken arm."

"Why are you unmarried?" the woman asked. "Or did you have a husband and not like him?"

"I am a priestess. I will not marry. The goddess decrees this so that I may best serve my people."

"We do not have so much gods here," the

woman said sympathetically. "We have *asabiyah*, the spirit of the tribe. It is the most estimable way of living. Our men go on raids very often against our enemies. Or against our friends when there are no enemies about. The women care for animals, make food, rugs, clothing, have babies. In this way, we keep *asabiyah*."

"And, does no one ever object to their role?"

"What is to object? A camel must be a camel. A monkey must be a monkey."

Shahiroz agreed there could be no arguing with the truth of this statement.

"But, what if a girl does not wish to marry? Or if she prefers to choose a husband for herself?"

"All young women desire to marry," the woman assured her. "But no girl is married against her will. It is her right to refuse her parents' choice. Mind you, then she must be killed."

The bustle continued through the morning. When the sun warmed even the shadiest spots, making limbs lazy and thoughts loll, the camp began to quiet. All sought a place to sleep away the early afternoon.

The young man led Shahiroz to a shady grove, scented with oranges. They sat close together under fragrant bows.

She begged for songs of the desert. He sang to

her of life spent in constant motion amid a vast, unyielding landscape. Sun-shattered dawns, fiery horizons at evenings and dunes glimmering in the moonlight, white as snow in the mountains. Beauty that conjures up yearning. The hunger of a man's soul for whatever might be found beyond the next rise. Beauty that completes and fulfills. A poem of a man and woman lying together under a purple night sky. She shivered with pleasure.

"I've heard at least a thousand songs in the temple. But never has a priest made me feel as you do."

"They do not sing as if they are making love."

"No," she whispered. "More like a prayer."

"When we find our beloved, they become the same thing," he said.

"Stay here," the young man urged. "We have no temple, so no fighting over who owns the gods."

" I have pledged myself to service."

"Pledge yourself to me. You'll forget about the goddess."

"Would you want that?"

"No," he admitted. "I want you as you are."

That evening, the desert wives and their guests gathered around a bonfire, sucking luscious ruby seeds from pomegranate halves, picking over the details of the day. The wedding had been splendid, opulent. The groom was majestic. Noble. A lusty stallion. The bride was radiant. Her neck dripped with silver. The wedding feast was sumptuous. There were prodigious smears on the tent flaps where the men wiped their fingers after eating. The Hebrew women must be overcome. They would hardly be believed when they related the wealth and hospitality of this tribe to the outside world.

The desert women crowed over noises from the marriage tent.

"This one isn't going to ground without a struggle."

"She should hold him off, until he begs to be inside her. First desire is always the most potent."

Singing from the men's side. Swaying bodies, silhouetted against the glow of bonfires. Deep laughter. Applause, which must indicate the performance of an accomplished poet.

A crone, bent, snake-skinned, told the women a tale of love. "A warrior, who had long been from home, found himself yearning for the embrace of his wife. He put a kiss on a date leaf and gave it to a hawk, instructing the bird to carry it to his wife, so she would remember his affection and remain faithful. At last, the man returned home to find that his wife had given birth to a daughter. 'See how great our love is?' the woman rejoiced. 'When I placed the leaf with your kiss to my lips, life leaped in my womb.' The warrior was outraged. 'How could this happen unless a man and woman lie together?' He could not bring himself to kill his wife, as was his right, but he banished her to the wilderness, demanding that she never return to his tents.

"The woman wandered, drinking dewfall from leaves of the acadia tree, keeping her baby alive by begging the small desert animals to bring what seeds and berries they could find. The girl grew up tall, beautiful, with eyes as gentle as a dove and lips as welcoming as dawn.

"After many years, a young prince was riding through the desert. He was a hero, brave as a lion, fearless before danger. But as soon as he saw the girl, his strength became as nothing. The gods themselves are not mightier than love. When he reached home, he lay on his bed, consumed with longing, shedding tears of blood.

"The queen became alarmed and sent soldiers into the desert to find the girl. He may not marry her, she thought. She is not a princess, or even a member of our tribe. But, he may spend one night with her, and be cured of this sickness.

"The soldiers brought the girl and her mother back to the tents of the prince. The girl's neck was hung with strands of pearls and sapphires. She was dressed in a robe embroidered in gold. Then, she was taken to the prince who jumped up, embraced her, and took her with eagerness and passion.

"The next morning, the prince's mother came to the bedchamber to remove the girl and send her back to the desert. There was nothing there but two perfect crimson roses, the colour of the desert sky after a storm. The woman ran to the girl's mother, demanding to know what had become of her son. The mother said, 'My daughter has been betrayed three times, by those who thought only of what they themselves desired. First, she was wronged by her father, who denied her. Then by you, who gave her to your son knowing full well that no man would want her once her purity was gone. And finally by your son, who took her without first asking if she herself wished it. My daughter, who has the strength of a desert plant, willed herself and your son into roses with thorns. She reminds us that desire is both pleasure and sharpness. It is as treacherous as it is beautiful.'

"The queen went away. And wept until she expired."

Shahiroz shared tales of the goddess. "In Babylon, they will be celebrating her feast day now. When the first barley ripens, we place kisses and wishes on rose petals, then toss them into the river.

The goddess holds a crescent, carved with thirteen lines, one for each moon cycle in a year, reminding us of the magical potency of renewal. Her left hand is on her belly, teaching us to caress ourselves lovingly, to know the place that is only for pleasure. Desire is an offering to the goddess. To awaken the life force is to call forth her blessing."

The desert women nodded and smiled, answering with low, lush songs of springs gushing from secret chasms. The circle joined hands, fingers entwining, moving their bodies to the music.

A late summer moon hung over the barrens, blood red as a ripened apple. The sky blazed, a temple of stars.

Shahiroz walked toward the scent of orange blossoms and the melody of a *rabab*. The young man rose from the shadow of a spreading tree, rugged, golden and commanding as a statue of Marduk, with eyes of lapis blue. He pulled down flowers, fragrant and fragile, for her thick black hair. His right arm embraced her. His left hand was under her head. Their breath awakened each other.

In the morning, Shahiroz's father appeared.

"There is turmoil in the camp. Where is Shahiroz?"

"Gone to bathe," her mother said.

"A young man of the tribe is saying he will marry

her. She is not of this tribe. She will never be presented at the house of his mother."

Shahiroz came, arms glistening with water.

"What have you done? You have disgraced us all."

"I have done nothing wrong."

"You have betrayed your family and insulted our hosts. He was betrothed to another girl, did you know that? No man will want her now and she will die of shame. The *shaykh* demands that you be brought before him. You must go down on your knees and beg forgiveness from the tribe."

"I have done nothing wrong," she repeated. "I am free to fulfill my Honour like any other woman."

"You will be punished for such whorishness," her father's voice shook with rage. "Your veil will be torn. You will be stripped bare and lashed. They know what loyalty is due the tribe here."

Her mother grabbed at his sleeve. "Surely, you will not allow him to harm her."

"I will do my best to keep the *shaykh* from beating her to death. They are within their rights to do so. I will promise to proclaim the praises of this tribe to the world outside with such accolades as have never been heard before."

"How can I help my daughter?" Her mother's words choked with fear.

"Pray to Yahweh on your knees that he may open the *shaykh's* heart and make him merciful. And, tell the women to pack their belongings. We must go before they decide to exact justice from all of us."

Shahiroz's mother began to shake the Hebrew women awake, "Get up, get up. We must leave today. We cannot trespass on our hosts' generosity any longer."

"We had thought to stay a week at least," the cry went up.

Shahiroz walked with her father.

"What will happen to the young man?" she asked.

"His own people will decide. Your transgression is all that concerns us."

"I wish to see him, to know he is unhurt."

"You are not in a position to seek a favour of any kind."

"I did nothing wrong. I may honour the goddess where I choose."

"Not here."

"If a thing is true, it is true everywhere."

"They are within their rights to have every one of us beaten."

"I committed no transgression. The goddess is never offended by love."

"There will be no more talk of the goddess. Do you understand me? I forbid it. I forbid you to tell her stories ever again. All who speak her name will be silenced. Those who observe her rites will be punished. I will plead with the *shaykh* to let you marry this young man and he will come with us."

"I will never marry. And I will not apologize."

"Can you not tell that I am trying to help you?"

"You're trying to help yourself."

"You've learned nothing. You don't even feel shame."

"I feel shame for you."

Her father's hand smacked hard across her cheek.

"God forgive me." His voice broke. He reached out to touch the place where her skin glowed red. Shahiroz pulled away sharply, pressing her lips together hard, willing herself not to crumble in tears of shock and pain. "God forgive me, Shahiroz," he sobbed. "I am so sorry. I am so sorry. This is not what I wanted to have happen."

"Yes. It is father," she said quietly. "It's exactly what you wanted to happen. Can you not see that?"

They had reached the tent. The flap was pushed open. And moments later, Shahiroz found that the rip of a whip across her naked back was not as searing as the glance of her father's palm across her face.

The travellers dragged their feet, gazing at endless barren steppe through scrub brush and past the ragged grey limbs of solitary trees. The air was so heavy with heat that the marchers gasped for breath. Weeks passed. Finally, no one could remember how long they had been walking. Or any world beyond this eternal wasteland.

Day by day, Shahiroz and her mother trudged silently.

Finally, "The salve will calm the worst of the wounds. Your flesh will hardly hurt in another few days."

No answer.

"Your father has instructed me to boil pomegranate and passion fruit leaves for a vaginal compress."

"My body is not tainted."

"And— he says you must take a new name. Something befitting a Hebrew woman."

Shahiroz remained silent.

"This is beyond my powers to heal, Shahiroz. I have nothing to give. No wisdom that might help you. No draughts that will calm their anger. No potion to still the fear."

The girl did not speak. Then a hand reached out, grasping her mother's tightly. They held on, tramping side by side. Fingers joined. "I have what I need, mother."

When the moon changed, the women did not gather to share stories and prayers. Fears were shared in hushed voices. Shahiroz's father announced that all would observe a time of remembrance. On this day, some sixty years earlier, the Babylonians had invaded Jerusalem. "This observance reminds us of our failure to live up to our sacred vocation. Just as the people of Moses lost faith in the desert and turned to worshipping a foreign god, so our breach of faith, allowing the worship of foreign idols in the temple, led to a breach in the walls of Jerusalem. Never again must we worship the gods of others or ally ourselves with the enemies of Yahweh."

"How did the mother become enemy?" The women whispered to each other as they lay down to sleep.

"The dome of the first temple seemed always about to lift into the air," an ancient muttered. "Ready to shoot up into the heavens from the sheer energy of the prayers said there. It wasn't praises to Yahweh alone that were offered."

"The men are saying that those who speak of the goddess will be dragged from the new temple. Women and children slain like beasts. Breasts cut off."

"We have always worshipped the mother together," the old woman answered. "The men will feel differently when we are in Jerusalem. They will honour tradition. After all, you cannot cut creation in half and expect it to be whole. Shahiroz said so. Be still now."

Shahiroz lay on her blanket, silent and apart. She had no stories to share, no assurances that all would be well. Through the past weeks, the sting of the whip marks on her back bled into the greater pain of loss. She felt the sharp ache of being useless to provide honest comfort or to give assurance to anxious fears.

Cold stars littered the heavens, plentiful as the white flowers that had blanketed the meadows outside Babylon. It was almost the month of Tishri. Far away, in the city left behind, preparations for the fall festival would be underway. Visitors would crowd the city once again. Vendors would pile their booths high with exotic offerings from the furthest corners of the world. The paving stones outside the temple and palace would be scrubbed to a glowing lustre. And the autumnal prayers of the goddess would be practised with diligence in the temple. Beautiful odes. Poetic lamentations. So glorious, the words often caught in the throats of the priests and priestesses as they rehearsed. Passionate.

Haunting. The goddess bidding farewell to her lover, weeping from her soul. Singing him gently, lovingly into death. At that moment, though the promise of rebirth is always present, it is the affliction of loss that charges the words with feeling, the wrenching, agonized keening of a heart whose sole desire seems lost forever.

Shahiroz curled her knees to her chest. She wept, being careful to do so quietly.

It was not the god who was dying. Not this time. And when the mother was gone, no priest or priestess would stand on the temple steps in Jerusalem, calling her back. Back to her lover. To passion and pleasure which are the province of springtime. Back to her children. To love and joy, which are the source of all life. Back to her place in the cycle of existence. The wheel of the year would continue turning, moved by the hand of a solitary god.

In that moment, Shahiroz recalled a story of the old goddess, Inanna, she had heard in the temple. Lying alone in the dark, she repeated it softly to herself.

A woman who had prayed for a child for many years was finally delivered, but the baby was dead. In a flood of tears, the woman took the baby before Inanna, begging the great goddess to restore life to her child. Inanna agreed, but only on the condition that, first, the woman complete one task; to go down to the village and bring back a single mustard seed from the first house she came to that had never been touched by death.

The woman rushed into town, knocking on the first door she came to and stating what she needed. But, the man who lived there said sadly that he couldn't help her. His old father had passed away just that day. The woman ran to the next house. But the old woman there said she had lost two sons in battle years ago. At the next house, a young wife had recently died in childbirth. At the next, they were grieving the death of their mother who passed away a year ago. At the next, they were mourning a sister.

No one could help her. Dejected and exhausted, the woman returned to Inanna to say she had failed in her task. She knew now that no household was untouched by death. The goddess consoled the woman for the loss of her child and promised her that, while she could not save her from the grief of loss which befalls all human beings, she would give her a greater gift. She would teach her what it was that could never be lost. She would teach her what endured. The woman stayed with Inanna, becoming a wise priestess, and then returned to her people.

Overhead, there was a wash of icy brilliance. The

scholars of Babylon who studied the heavens, the wisest astronomers in the world, believed that some stars were quite new, almost as recent as humankind. Others were nearly as old as the gods. Soon, they would wink out of existence, leaving newer lights to brighten the night sky. It was the way of the universe itself to change, the way of life to suffer loss. Her mother had anticipated the loss of her profession when they were in Babylon. The gift of healing with herbs was precious to her, just as the call to heal with prayers and stories was to her daughter.

Shahiroz stood up quietly, careful not to disturb those sleeping nearby. She crept through the lines of slumbering bodies, finally picking out the form of her mother. Gently, she lay down beside, whispering her awake.

"What endures?" Shahiroz asked. "What is there that I can hold on to, that never alters or ends? No matter what happens."

She could see her mother's slow thoughtful smile even in the darkness.

"Maybe only my love for you."

Regretfully, "You wanted me to be a priestess."

"You always will be."

"Without a temple?"

"The goddess' true sanctuary has no walls. A

very wise priestess, who is also my daughter, told me that."

Shahiroz huddled closer.

"My mistress in the temple once told us that faith is like a rope. It's easy to trust it will hold if we're only using it to tie up a bundle. What if you have to hang from it over a precipice? Only in matters of life and death do we know the true strength of our beliefs."

"And what do you believe?"

"That the mother does not forget her children. I am sure of it. As sure as I am that day comes after night."

"We're healers, Shahiroz. We give what we can, and trust in time and the gods to do the rest. Balance will return."

"And spring will forever follow winter. Though we cannot know when it will come."

Tenderly, Shahiroz wrapped her arms around her mother. And wept herself to sleep.

Wilderness. Stony plains. Parched, brittle trees. Days spent huddled under low ridges, shawls or blankets wrapped tightly around the eyes and mouths, as the desert winds roared and sand blew high as ocean waves. Unrelieved plodding beneath unchanging stars, limbs barely sustaining the body's weight. Sometimes a pause, to rest for a day or two, if a bit of water or slice of shade was found. Not enough to refresh the body or revive the spirit. A traveller would collapse, or not wake at nightfall. Shahiroz would assist her mother in applying a few precious drops of water to lips and eyelids, or else would fold the arms gently, motioning the men to scavenge for gravestones. The journey resumed. Exhaustion extinguished the energy to mourn.

When they reached Damascus, the women did not go in to market. The eyes of scarecrows stared from under dirt-caked head shawls toward smoke rising from the city. The men obtained fresh water and a little fruit, which were tasted without pleasure.

They were almost home. Shahiroz's father was tireless in his efforts to keep them moving, bustling from one end of the group to the other. Admonishing, cajoling, for forty years, their forbearers had wandered in the wilderness, sustained by the unfailing companionship of Yahweh, before being brought safely and at last to the Promised Land. Their own journey had been only a few months, a summer, an autumn. What cause for despair when the trek was so short and their destination now so near?

Dry thorns and blistered rocks. The road from Damascus stretched dusty and unchanging as the desert. Then, gaunt stone houses appeared, lapped in dust, strewn across rubbled hillsides. Late evening sun bathed white stone roofs in gold. On surrounding hills, high up, the soil glowed darker. Small orchards dotted the landscape, patches of deep green. Then, in the far distance, the mountains of Moab, looming bronzed and dusky over the deep hollow of the Dead Sea.

And suddenly, rising before them in the narrow rift valley, golden brown as the rock it grew out of, a walled city.

"*Yerah Shalom*," the cry went up. "Jerusalem. We are home."

Shadows cloaked the ravages of destruction and awakened an ancient spell.

Men, women and children fell to their knees.

"Great is Yahweh," Shahiroz's father proclaimed joyously.

"And greatly to be praised in the city of our
god, amid the mountains of our holiness.
Beautiful, the joy of all the earth is this mount
of Zion and the city of the great king.
Thy praises shall be heard unto the ends of the
earth.
Let mount Zion rejoice with us. Let your
daughters of Judah be glad.
For Yahweh is our god forever and ever."

Rejoicing. Men and boys linked arms, hurling each other about in a wild dance of celebration. Women wept, laughed. Holding high the babies who had been born on the journey. Crying, "Home. My heart. My miracle. This is home." Rapturous hymns of praise mingled with songs of jubilant victory. Yahweh had led them from the chains of captivity, guided and sustained them through the perilous journey. The time for the fulfillment of his great plan was at hand.

The light faded. Gilded rooftops were lost in darkness. Women kindled fires. Limbs found new strength. Old folk clapped and laughed, keeping time with the whirling steps of dancers. Psalms were shouted and sung until voices could bless no more. Merriment echoed across the black stony hillsides. No one thought of sleeping. The festivities continued through the night.

With the approach of dawn, the men began eagerly discussing who should go into Jerusalem to announce their arrival. Before a party could be organized, or petitions finalized, a scout arrived from the city. The man spoke with a thick inflection, different from the Hebrew they knew. The men from Babylon pushed close, eager to assure him of their identity. The man looked skeptical. These weren't any family he knew.

The man was invited to eat. The women, springing to life, scrounged the last of their provisions into a passable meal. He chewed casually, was even seen to raise his eyebrows at something gone slightly off or that was not to his taste. The onlookers were shocked. They had forgotten the luxury of preference months before.

As the man dined, Shahiroz's father sat close, explaining their journey. "Truly, Yahweh is the greatest of all gods. He moved the heart of Cyrus, returning us to our brothers, just as he moved the heart of the Pharaoh, freeing our people under our ancestor, Moses." The man grunted.

"Yahweh directs us to re-build his kingdom and to re-establish his law."

"Are you saying we haven't had laws all this time?" the man asked.

"Of course our brothers and sisters have obeyed as best as they could. But without your priests … your teachers and leaders …"

The man wiped his jaw. "Been serving a foreign king all this time, and you want to tell us how to live like Israelites?"

"To work together to re-establish the glory of Yahweh. Our nation. The authority of the temple."

"Ten thousand men died building the first one. And it wasn't your lot, it was ours, the farmers and labourers. There's many who consider we're better off paying taxes to the Babylonians or Persians and being left in peace, than to the Hebrew priests who owned all the land, taxed us to work it, and still meddled in our ways at the end of the day." He stretched and yawned. "So, this is the way of it. I've been sent to tell you that we've no inclination to have our brothers, as you call yourselves, back in our city. Yahweh will have to free you to re-establish his glory elsewhere."

"It's our home." A shout from thc crowd.

"Sixty years ago, maybe. It's the way of things to change." He looked over toward the clutch of women. "Might there be a priestess among you?"

Shahiroz stepped forward.

The man nodded respectfully. "The fall festival commences soon. We'd be most honoured if you would come and lead us in the lamentations. It will be a great blessing to hear the prayers of the goddess said in Hebrew once more." He rose. "As for the rest, we'll send out some food. You won't starve on our doorstep." He walked off into the night.

Silence.

Then, a roar of anguish went up, the people wailing with a single voice. It was unbearable, to have come so far and to have suffered so greatly, to have left home on the promise of a more perfect home, only to be turned away at journey's end. The fury became moans of despair. They would starve. There was nowhere to go. No one was obliged to accept them.

They would fall in their tracks if forced to walk again.

Then anger. They were denied their rightful positions. Treated like beggars in their own homeland.

The hills echoed with rage and with painful longing, plaintive as the wail of a ram's horn. They were children of Jerusalem, sons and daughters of this land. Who could deny them their birthright?

Shahiroz's father called above the riot, "Our god has made a promise to his people. We do not forget the praise and faithfulness we owe to Yahweh. Yahweh will not desert us. He will lead us into Jerusalem. He will champion us in rebuilding the temple so his name may be worshipped by all generations. We will send a priestess to the city. One who can talk to the people and move their hearts. She will speak for us and for Yahweh and return our brothers to their senses."

"Shahiroz," they called out, "Blessed is Shahiroz. A saviour among us."

"Shahiroz will serve us," her father assured them all loudly, "as she has always done. Be patient. Trust in Yahweh. Soon we will march, triumphant, into the city as Yahweh has promised."

Shahiroz's father held out his hand toward her.

Her mother grasped at her sleeve and whispered, "What will you do, daughter?"

"I will trust in the goddess," she answered quietly. "I will have faith that spring will come again."

Priest and priestess walked apart, far up a slope covered in rocky stubble. Her father wearily mounted a high boulder. Shahiroz bent down, picking up a smooth cinnamon-coloured pebble, holding it gently in her palm.

"Has your back healed?" he asked.

"Yes."

"It no longer pains you?"

"Not often."

"Blessed is Yahweh, who brings healing to the broken."

He sat for a long time without speaking again, staring off at the dim lights of the city below.

Finally, "When we were marched into Babylon, I remarked to my old father that the air seemed drenched in jasmine. He answered that the air of Jerusalem is drenched in prayers, which are sweeter still."

He turned to her. "Foxes breed amid the rubble of the ruined temple, Shahiroz. Did you know?"

She shook her head.

"When you go into the city, you will see the remains of a great aquaduct, a sluice, tall as the Ishtar Gate. Water diverted from streams in far-off hills once gushed down its channel, to the old temple site, where it was used to wash away the blood of sacrifices. There are no rivers here, you see. One could hear the rush of water flowing down from the most remote alcoves in the temple. It was miraculous engineering. You'd have thought the gods alone could have contrived it. Took seventy years to complete. The whole working life of some of the fathers and sons chosen to build it. Do you know why they committed themselves to such a task?"

"I expect our leaders told them to."

"Well yes, some," her father conceded. "But I believe for others it was the idea of a life's work dedicated to something that would endure. Serving the people of their own time, certainly, but also far into the future when those who built it, those who knew them, were long erased from the landscape. It's a great thing. To believe that there is something that endures and to devote one's life to it." Her father looked away from the lights, into the deep blanket of desert. "We're a small people, we Hebrews. Insignificant. Helpless among the powers of this world. It would be easy for us to disappear like the temple, to crumble and finally scatter like pebbles in a sandstorm."

"Surely, that is unlikely."

"I have served two mighty nations, Shahiroz. Babylon, Persia. Neither cared if we lived or died, except we could be used for their purpose. And I have studied and served in the greatest temple on earth. The most learned priests, the most ancient teachings, the most venerated wisdom on the mysteries of the universe. Yet, ask any of those faithful, scholarly men what is the nature of the gods, or the soul, and not one of them can say for certain. I will tell you. This life force, this power unseen, it is what it is. Our little minds can know nothing of it. The wisest man is the one who admits that.

Still, we continue to believe that whatever this power may be, it cares about the world of men and about our troubles. Perhaps we have no other way of making sense of our lives. We are taught to believe that we are god's greatest creation, yet I have come to consider that he is ours. That we imagine the gods in ways that will speak to the troubles we have. It's all we can do. Tell stories that say how we believe this world must be run."

"To help people to feel safe and loved."

"I suppose so. Well, we Hebrews are neither. We must save ourselves, for no one else will come to our aid. We must tell stories of a god that loves and protects us, one who can save us from being swallowed up. Our brothers in Jerusalem have not seen the vastness of the world beyond, as we have. They cannot know how tenuous the continuance of our people might be.

"You have the gift to speak in a way that inspires faith and trust. Persuade the people of this city that only one vision of god may serve us now. Yahweh alone may be crowned in Jerusalem. Save us, Shahiroz, or foxes will play among the rubble of our graves as well. The name of the children of Jerusalem will vanish like morning mist."

The sky lightened. Black washed into grey, grey into pink. Scarlet streaks burned across the boulders where they sat. The sun blossomed over the old city like a rose.

"I cannot choose between loyalty to the mother or to her children."

"Her stories do not serve us now."

"She has always been with us. Honoured and adored everywhere. If it were not so, you would not have to resort to threats to suppress her worship."

"People forget, Shahiroz, faster than you think. In another sixty years they'll no longer recall any but Yahweh. In a hundred, they will believe that his stories and laws had no origin other than that they sprang from acts of history and the lips of the god himself."

Shahiroz stood, gazing at the view unfolding before her. In the distance, the barren coastline of the Dead Sea was barely visible in the morning haze. Silvery pigeons dipped below fiery opal clouds. On one side, the harsh stony mountains of arid desert, painted fuchsia by rising light. On the other, deep shadowy green hills promising figs, wine, milk and honey. In the centre, the shattered walls of the old city was washed with the colour of blood. And within, glowing crimson, a great rock platform topped by jagged teeth of stone that had once been a temple. In this spot, her father assured them, creation was begun and Adam was born of dust. And here was the place where their people could breathe new life.

Slowly, she turned over the pebble in her hand.

"There is a story of Asherah…"

"I do not wish to hear that name."

"Just this time. One last tale. A woman came to the goddess, saying she had fallen in love with a wonderful man who returned her devotion. She begged Asherah for the secret of how to keep this love, and all things that are precious, from dropping away. The goddess instructed the woman to pick up a stone from the ground. Like the one I have here." She opened her fingers and showed the small golden orb.

"Shahiroz, I have forbidden you to …"

"Listen. Then, Asherah asked the woman to show her the best way to hang onto the stone. Immediately, the woman clutched the pebble in her hand as tightly as she could. But, of course, she couldn't manage this for long. Her fingers tired. The stone dropped to the ground. The goddess instructed the woman to pick the stone up again. She told her to turn her hand upward and place the stone on her open palm. The woman realized that this way she might hold onto the stone forever. Only by not grasping could she hope to keep the things she loved."

"Well," her father rose stiffly. "An interesting tale. Now, I must go back down and share some stories that will be of more use. Offer reassurance. Promise faithfulness. The story of Moses parting the Red Sea is helpful, I think. Deliverance when all hope is gone. I do not blame you, Shahiroz. Who knows, perhaps in sixty years, the world will have forgotten us anyway. Even with the stories of Yahweh to protect us."

"I will make you a bargain," Shahiroz said quickly. "One small promise, in return for which I will do what you desire."

He stopped.

"Tell the tales of your solitary god, father. Write them down. Let them protect our people and keep us true to who we are. Let them become the roots that nurture and sustain us. But, allow me to place a story of Her among them. Just one little tale. A whisper of who she is and what she once meant to us. So that if the time comes, when our troubles change again, and we need a new way to know the divine, we may find her."

"Others will write the books, Shahiroz. Many hands and hearts will ..."

"If they sense truth, something will remain. A seed in the desert sand. A pebble in an open palm. That is all I ask. In return, I will not take a husband. And I will never change my name. But, I will go into the city. I will speak for Yahweh."

Her father nodded. He plodded off down the bank.

The young woman stood on the hillside. The first radiance dissolved into honeyed haze above the city. She recalled the moment, a lifetime ago, when she had stood on the step of the Esaglia Temple. The sun had been this brilliant, had glittered off the walls of the courtyard as blinding as over the stones of the city below her now. She remembered the rush of certainty that had surged through her body, bringing words to sooth a grieving and uncertain crowd. Words of assurance and faithfulness. Hope.

"Where there is springtime, she is always with us." Rays of light warmed her face, drying her tears. "The goddess does not forget her children. Even when we seem to have forgotten her." Soft wind against her cheek, soothing as her mother's caress.

Shahiroz reached out her arms.

"Divine Mother. Mistress of mankind. Lover, sister, guide.
Pillar of your people.
Springtime for the soul.
Lay down the burden of care for your children.
Your children of Jerusalem sing with gratitude and love.
Rest.
Be our peace in the quiet earth.
Our peace in the shining stars.
Fall from our thoughts, softly, as the leaves float to the ground.
Autumn passes into winter, winter into spring.
The vines will grow, new grass appear,
And the scent of lilies will resurrect a waiting world.
Then we will call to you, as you have called to us.
You, who dwell in a garden,

Listen for our voice.

And awaken us to your presence once more."

Shahiroz lowered her arms. "And please Mother, please. Do not forget your daughter."

Then she went down, to where her people waited.

IV

Peter Miller sat at his desk on Friday morning, head in hands. It was over. His plans for updating the library computer system, adding more teaching assistants, refurbishing the lunchroom chairs. The hallways would not be jam-packed come fall, with eager paying students, anxious to learn at the feet of religious academia's newest queen. Grants would not pour down like holy wine. The college would simply sink into permanent obscurity. Their theological opinions would be as much sought after as those of The Sacred Order of Lawn Bowling Druids.

The police had turned up nothing. "We contacted Professor Niefeild's wife two nights ago." They insisted. "He was spotted playing baseball." Then, a couple matching their description was reportedly discovered in a seedy area of town, lying naked together in a community garden plot. The police settled for a warning, and considered the case closed.

Peter pressed palms to forehead. There was a crash in the hallway. Lucy and Reggie staggered in, falling against each other, giggling. They were fully dressed.

"Thank god! Everyone's already here!"

The small college chapel was agreeably full. Peter pushed Lucy toward the lectern, nodding to the dean, beaming at the religious press.

Lucy, glowing, dishevelled, turned to face her audience.

"Any questions?" she asked brightly.

"Well ... could you tell us what your book is about?"

"Of course. It's about bad art. I mean, really, really bad art. Divine mother? Stick figures, smiling passively. They look about as delighted and engaged in the great cosmic dance of bliss as someone passing a kidney stone."

Silence.

"Um, could you elaborate on the theological model of, uh... kidney stones?"

"Not without boring myself to tears."

"Well, then could you tell us about... about... anything?"

Lucy laughed. "The point is you shouldn't pay so much attention to what I've said in this book. I'm certainly not planning to. I mean, what theological dunce came up with the notion that the sacred could ever be separated from life and passion and helpless joy? And don't get me started on this long-suffering nonsense. Personally, I'd rather be known for what I wouldn't put up with, than what I would. Poor stiff, timid little goddesses." Lucy leafed through the copy before her and sighed regretfully. "What on earth did we do to you? And that lonely male god… Anyway," she tossed the book aside, "it's bad art. I just didn't realize it before. Sorry about that. And now," she smiled gloriously. "For what does matter. I'm going to take you all to see a garden."

Lucy held out a hand to Reggie, who accepted it gratefully. Together, they led a trail of bewildered hopeful religion writers out of the chapel, through the big wooden front doors.

Peter Miller stared out the window in the empty place of worship.

Sometime later, a tall young woman with black fluffy hair appeared in the doorway.

"Principal Miller?" She came beside him. "I'm Rosie Banks. I'm Professor Niefeild's new teaching assistant."

"I doubt he'll be needing an assistant." Impossible not to sound downright mournful. "He no longer appears to be teaching."

"Well, I heard that. And what happened here today. Though, any religious scholar worth a rat's ass would have seen it coming. I mean that respectfully, of course."

Peter nodded, without rancor.

"But the thing is, this might have been my doing. Or partly my doing. You see, I told Professor Niefeild the answer."

Peter nodded again, not understanding.

"Why *Song of Songs* is in the Bible. I told him what it's there for."

Peter Miller chuckled. "Professor Niefeild is an acknowledged expert in the field, Miss Banks. Years of research. Six authoritative books. Another on the way. There's really nothing you could have told him that he wouldn't have already..."

"Let me explain," the young woman said.

When she finished and had gone again, Peter Miller reached over, pushing the window wide, breathing in a distinct perfume of lilies. "I think ...," he began. He stopped, picked up his jacket, shut the chapel doors behind him, and strode out of Hosanna College, whistling.

When spring had passed, and throughout the long hot summer, Reggie and Lucy spent their days in the garden, sleeping outside until the lure of a bed and shower became too much for them. They urged the old man to come home with them as well, but he proclaimed himself content where he was.

Beans grew long tendrils, entwining themselves around stakes or cascading over the ground like the sweep of a woman's hair. Cucumbers burst their skins, corn stalks stood erect through sweltering days and crisp nights. Strawberries appeared with their fragrant red flesh, staining Lucy and Reggie's lips and fingers as they stood, rejoicing, over the first harvest. Lettuce and peppers plumped up round and firm. Sunflowers blazed. Eggplants ripened, purple as the night sky over the desert. Pea blossoms glowed like tiny stars.

The men in nice suits returned to taste tomatoes. They smacked their lips appreciatively and grinned with pleasure. Lucy and Reggie gathered seeds from empty stems, placing them in white envelopes to be tucked away for winter.

When the evenings turned cool, the two sat wrapped together in one blanket. The old man slowly combed through withered leaves and crumbling vines, searching for the last cherry tomatoes or summer peas.

"They start the Out Of The Cold program next

week," he said. "Bed and Breakfast. Time to go back inside." He ambled off around the side of the cathedral.

"What will we do?" Reggie asked Lucy.

"Go back to the college." She nestled closer in the deepening darkness. "Back to our students. Our hands full of ripe figs, pomegranates and myrrh. With stories to share."

"Tales of a new god?"

"A divine, who has only ever wanted for you and me to make love in a garden."

On the steps of the church, the old man sat talking softly to a young woman with dark fluffy hair. They spoke of the garden, how lush and verdant it had been this year, teeming with life and sweetness. Then they talked about the approaching cold, and when spring might come again. The young woman stood up. She leaned over, kissing the man tenderly on the lips.

"You were a long time," he noted.

She laughed gaily, and walked off into the gathering night.

The old man pulled his coat close around his aging body, lay his head down on the stone cathedral step, and drifted into sleep.

AUTHOR'S NOTES

The setting

The ancient city of Babylon has been extensively excavated and many documents have been uncovered, inscribed on tablets. Given the virtually indestructible nature of clay when dried and particularly when baked, this means that an enormous number of these writings have survived into present time. While a great many are concerned with mundane matters of trade and commerce, royal dictates, military accounts, prayers, incantations, stories and descriptions of rituals also remain. We are blessed with great riches when it comes to learning of the culture and structure of this remarkable place.

The layout of the city is roughly as I have presented it. Babylon was situated between the Tigris River on the east and Euphrates to the west, in the area now called Iraq. The Ishtar Gate stood at the north end, the grand Processional Way beginning at its doors, running through the centre of town and connecting with gates in the southern walls. The only major alteration I made was in placing the palace closer to the Esaglia Temple, halfway along the Processional Way, rather than across from the E-mah, which is more likely where it stood. In addition to the Esaglia, there was a temple called the Temple of the New Year located near the Ishtar Gate that may also have been a focal point during the Akitu Festival.

Babylon was filled with shrines and temples. Two sets of fortifying walls surrounded the city and were considered wonders of the ancient world. There is no definitive evidence, however, of the location or existence of the legendary Hanging Gardens or of any immense tower that may have served as the inspiration for the fabled Tower of Babel.

Biblical references to Babylon claim that its citizenry was particularly immoral. The author of *Revelation* labels the city, "Mother of Harlots, and the Abominations of the Earth." Nothing in my research indicated that the populace was in fact any more or less wicked than anywhere else.

The Akitu Festival

There is extensive historical documentation of this annual celebration of the New Year. References dating back to 979 BC indicate that it was a prominent and ancient event even at that time, the blessing of the gods being considered essential to the continuing well-being of the country. The story of King Nabonidus leaving the city for ten years, bringing the festival to a halt, is true.

By the 6th C BC, the festival was twelve days in length. I have tried to present the sequence and specifics of events as accurately as possible. Either a recitation or performance of the *enuma elish*, the so-called Epic of Creation, likely took place on the fourth day of the celebration. This was not the only Babylonian story of creation but, clocking in at about seven hours in length, it was certainly the longest. The attributes and symbols attributed to Ishtar and Marduk are historically documented. The ritual of the goddess bowing down before the priest/god is a fabrication. There are reliable accounts of the ritual shaming of the king, a grand parade of god figures and a union of the king and a priestess representing god and goddess. It is possible that this partnering originally involved actual intercourse, but by the time of this story it was sufficient for the pair to participate in a purely symbolic coupling. There is considerable evidence that the spring festival was once centred on the worship of the goddess but was gradually co-opted into a celebration of the powers of the god.

Priestesses and ritual prostitution

Women were certainly employed in positions of authority in the temples. Typically, priestesses did not marry, but were allowed to take lovers that might include long-term relationships. There is some evidence of priestesses having paid sex with worshippers.

The custom of women, other than those employed as religious, having sexual intercourse with a stranger at the temple in return for a coin is historically documented for this time period. It seems possible that this practice was common in many places. Titling this ritual the "Honour" is my creation.

Responsible scholars now caution against judging practices of ritual sexuality by modern Western standards of morality. The ritual joining of two people was a sacred act. The passion of the couple was thought to arouse the life force in the earth, to stir the gods into blessing the world with fertility and abundance. Combined spiritual and physical ecstasy was a means of connecting with the divine. It was a profoundly holy gesture. It would probably get a whole lot more people into church as well.

Similarly, the sacrifice of animals was not so much a carnal event as a gift of the beast's spirit and soul to the gods. The Biblical denouncement of ritual intercourse may have been part of the attempt to confine Jewish sexual activity to sanctioned intertribal marriage.

The Jews in captivity

Babylon came into its full glory during the reign of Nebuchadrezzar II (604–562 BC), who commissioned most of the architectural wonders for which the city became famous. It is also Nebuchadrezzar who was responsible for sacking Jerusalem twice, finally laying waste to the temple in 602 BC and bringing the elite of the city, the scholars, priests, wealthy and their families, to Babylon. It seems likely that only 10 to 20 percent of the total population of Jerusalem was exiled.

Removing the religious and political elite of a conquered city was a standard Babylonian tactic. Not only did this serve to keep potential troublemakers, the local leaders, under close control, it allowed for their indoctrination into Babylonian culture and education. The Jews in Babylon seemed to have been, for the most part, very well treated. There are records of food rations and housing being provided, as well as evidence of the exiles being employed in the temple and palace (some in places of considerable importance) and their sons sent to school. They were allowed to practice their own religion and retain their own language. Having said that, it is likely the exiles would have taken part in all formal observances of Babylonian religion. Gods were still largely considered attached to specific territories and regions and it was not uncommon to recognize and honour the gods of other nations along with our own when you were on alien soil.

There is evidence that a considerable number of intermarriages took place between Jews and Babylonians. This, along with the active participation of the exiles in the life of the city, must have caused concern for the continuance of their religion and culture among the leaders of the captives. It seems likely that this group would have considered themselves the fire tenders of the only legitimate form of Judaism. They must have worried as well that, without their presence in Jerusalem, control of the shrines and ritual offices, the province of their families for generations, would fall to the peasantry. While the Jews in Babylon had every reason to fret over their potentially permanent loss of power, prestige and money, I believe theirs was fundamentally a spiritual yearning. They were strangers in a strange land, longing for the life and god of their homeland.

Those left behind in Israel were the farmers and most basic labourers. It is unlikely that they had the means to rebuild the city and must have continued to live amid a ravaged landscape of toppled towers and a ruined temple. On the plus side, the Babylonians did not colonize Jerusalem and the official put in charge of the area either sold or gave outright land and vineyards to the poor who remained. This would have been an almost unimaginable boon to farmers who for generations had worked and paid rent and tariffs on land owned by the upper classes. I was unable to find any reliable information as to what actually occurred when the original landowners returned from exile. My supposition is that it wasn't all roses.

The Bible records that the Jews cheered the arrival of Cyrus' army in 539 BC. There is no historic account to back this up, though it does seem possible that Cyrus captured the city in a single day, which suggests little resistance if not an actual welcome. Cyrus chose the middle of the Akitu Festival to attack Babylon, so the fact that the city was in the throes of the biggest celebration of the year may have contributed to both the ease of his success and the warmth of the greeting.

Cyrus allowed the Jews to leave in 537 BC, possibly because he anticipated war with Egypt and wanted Jerusalem manned by those loyal to Persia when enemy armies marched through on their way to Babylon. Other than one statement in the Bible, there is no record of Cyrus providing funds specifically for the rebuilding of the temple in Jerusalem. Nor is there any evidence of the existence of a letter of royal decree indicating that this was the king's desire. There is historical documentation that some Jews chose to remain in Babylon and others migrated to surrounding cities, or as far away as Egypt where there was a significant Jewish population, rather than returning to Jerusalem. The route described for the return of the Jews to Jerusalem is the one most likely preferred by the Babylonians when they brought their captives home.

The Origins of the Bible

There is no conclusive evidence as to when the Jewish scriptures[1] were first written or compiled. There are, however, some persuasive arguments for its creation at the time of the Babylonian exile. One is the clarity and accuracy of Biblical accounts relating to this time period.

There is no proof that many of the events chronicled in the Jewish scriptures actually ever happened. There is no substantiating evidence, for example, of the claim that a mass exodus of Israelites left Egypt during the period indicated and significant proof that a large population of Jews remained living in Egypt throughout much of its history. The suggestion then is that this event, if it occurred at all, was far enough in the past for the specifics to have been forgotten or to have been subject to significant revision.

---

1 The Jewish Bible is also called the Hebrew or Jewish scriptures or Tanakh. Many Christians and Jews worry that the title "Old Testament" suggests that the Christian New Testament in someway replaces or improves on what went before. Also, I have chosen to use BC and AD throughout this book. More inclusive, but less commonly used designations are BCE (before common era) and CE.

However, historical records do exist that confirm the Biblical claim that the Jews were brought into exile during the reign of Nebuchadrezzar, released by Cyrus and that they returned to Jerusalem some time around 537 BC. The accuracy of the Biblical account leads scholars to speculate that this may indicate when the work was first compiled. The facts of the exile were clear, and so likely current in the minds of those chronicling the event. In addition to this, my contention is that the first books of the Bible may well have been compiled at this time because the vision of god and god's mission contained in them speaks with perfection to the specific challenges facing the returning Jews. This was the ideal book for the time.

The group of Jewish priests/scholars who put this work together is now commonly referred to as the "Deuteronomist Circle." This is just a fancy name for "the bunch of guys who put together the first part of the Old Testament." Their efforts resulted in a canon of nine books: *Genesis*, *Exodus*, *Leviticus*, *Numbers*, *Deuteronomy*, *Joshua*, *Judges*, *Samuel* (later divided into two parts by medieval Christian theologians) and *Kings*. There is evidence that *Song of Songs* may have been added almost immediately and that it remained as the final book for some time. Much as I'd love to believe this, given the story I've told here, I have to say I think the jury is not only still out about this, it's anticipating having to order in dinner. The Jewish scriptures continued to be revised and added to up to the first century AD.

Most tales that make it into religious canon are so widely known and so ancient they cannot be said to belong to any one group alone. Some of the stories and psalms chosen for inclusion in the Bible may have been borrowed and adapted from those of other tribes and religions. The story of the Great Flood is found in the Babylonian *Epic of Gilgamesh*, written centuries before the arrival of the Jews in that city. It was assumed into Hebrew lore and history. The *Ludlul bel nemeqi* named for its opening line, "I will praise the lord of wisdom," dates to the Kassite dynasty in Babylon (c. 1157–1570 BC) and bears striking resemblance to the book of *Job*. Many psalms clearly echo prayers offered to gods other than Yahweh and to goddesses, but alterations have been made to reflect the theological model of a single, male god.

The stories of Ishtar and Asherah

The stories Shahiroz tells are ones I have borrowed, adapted and stolen outright from every possible source. Where nothing of use could be found, I made up what I needed.

However, the Jewish observance of *Rosh Hodesh* or Festival of the New Moon is based on truth (and continues to this day, though not in this form) and the story connected with it here is from the Talmud.

The Book of Norea

This is a twelve-page rambling creation story that presents Yahweh and the female in a significantly different light than we see in the Old or New Testaments. It was discovered in a clay jar in the middle of the Egyptian desert in 1945, near the village of Nag Hammadi. It is written in Greek and was later translated into Coptic and dated 4TH C AD. There is no evidence whatsoever that it might have existed or been known in any form as early as the 6TH C BC. To learn more about this book, I recommend *Searching The Scriptures, A Feminist Commentary*, edited by Elisabeth Schüssler Fiorenza.

I used the *Book of Norea* as an allusion to the many stories and writings that must have existed but which the Old Testament editors chose not to make use of. It seems possible that some might well have presented other views of the roles and value of women and the nature of god than what we have in the Bible.

Herbal remedies and women healers

Most of the medicines and their uses listed in this work are taken from historical research. One exception is the claim that a combination of dried and ground acadia leaves mixed with camel's milk will cure constipation. Don't try that one. I made it up. There is extensive documentation of women serving as healers both officially and unofficially in this period of history. The increasing limitations placed on women healers are a device of this story and likely occurred later. It is clear, however, that women's rights in areas of property ownership, inheritance, etc. were becoming increasingly curtailed during the Babylonian/Persian period, so it seemed reasonable to suggest that their professional opportunities might be becoming more limited as well.

The desert people

No reliable records exist of the culture and beliefs of the desert nomads of 500 BC. I have based my portrayal loosely but I hope not entirely unfaithfully on the lives of more recent Bedouin tribes.

Goddess worship and the shift to a "one god" system

Ishtar is only one of the many possible names for the goddess. I have chosen to use it almost exclusively to avoid confusion.

Some of the prayers in this book are direct translations of the Babylonian originals or are a combination of several prayers condensed into a single piece.

There is evidence that the Babylonian and Persian systems of religion were slowly beginning to favour a monotheistic image of god. This does not mean they became wholly monotheistic however, as many gods were still worshipped even after they were all brought loosely under the umbrella of Marduk. There is significant evidence to suggest that the Jews of the first temple period worshipped the goddess as well as the god, on the temple site. The fall festival, a tribute to the dying god, is said to have taken place on a terrace adjoining the main building.

It is impossible to know for certain what factors led to the demise and demonizing of the feminine divine and the female imaging of god. My contention here is that economic and social pressures facing the Jews upon their return to Jerusalem played a significant role. However, this was not the work of a few months or years, but a concerted campaign over many decades or even centuries. What is clear is that the Old Testament writers attacked goddess worship with astounding viciousness, indicating:

- Goddess worship was widespread.
- Her followers were devoted. Extreme means, often brutality, were required to deter them.
- The feminine divine represented some kind of significant threat to the increasingly male-dominated social or economic order.

Readers with a particular interest in this topic cannot do better than to read *When God Was a Woman*, by Merlin Stone. There is significant evidence to suggest that worship of the goddess continued to occur in Jerusalem in both private and public ceremonies after the rebuilding of the temple. Those seeking Old Testament citations of goddess worship and its suppression should see *Under Every Green Tree: Popular Religion in Sixth Century Judah* by Susan Akerman.

Remnants of goddess worship are all around us. My own faith, Christianity, is particularly rich with allusions to her. The Christian celebration of Easter takes its name from the feast of a spring goddess of fertility and abundance. Many Catholic saints were local goddesses who were simply "Christianized." There is evidence that church-sanctioned veneration of the Virgin Mary was a response to the impossibility of persuading the masses to give up their much-loved feminine deities. Interestingly, there are significantly more Catholic churches dedicated to Mary than to Christ. And, anyone who has stood in church at Christmas and sung "The Holy and the Ivy" has participated in continuing the story of the dying god.

Oscar Wilde said, "Truth, in matters of religion, is simply the opinion that has survived." And, in his seminal work *The Great Code*, Northrope Frye reminds us not to consider change in matters of religious observance and thought to be one and the same as advancement. Lay these observations side by side and I wonder, in this great truth of god as being both solitary and male, what have we lost? And what is there about the goddess that we just can't seem to completely let go of?

Song of Songs

Part of the five *megillot* (which simply means "scrolls"), *Song of Songs* is grouped with the books of *Ruth*, *Lamentations*, *Ecclesiastes* and *Esther* in the Jewish scriptures, coming after *Job* and before *Ruth*. In the Protestant Old Testament *Song of Songs* is placed between Ecclesiastes and Isaiah. Opinion is divided as to whether the work is a single continuous piece or a cycle of poems, by one author or from a variety of sources.

Almost every Christian theologian of every age explains *Song of Songs* as a description of Christ's relationship to the church or the Logos (Word) to the soul. Considerable effort is often made to distance the work from any connection to physical love or earthly desire. In Jewish scholarship, it's often described as a metaphysical marriage between Yahweh and the Children of Israel. These views have considerable attraction. There is a mystical quality to the poem, one that has inspired religious thinkers and dreamers through the ages. Rabbi Akiba proclaimed *Song of Songs* the "holy of holies" and Martin Luther called it *das Hohelied*, "the high song." Saint Theresa of Avila and Saint John of the Cross, both 16TH century Spanish religious figures, each meditated on *Song of Songs*, resulting in some of Theresa's most profound visions and John's most eloquent poetry. It has been suggested, in fact, that it is the life-affirming energy of the piece that gave John the strength to endure torture and imprisonment.

Only in the last few decades have scholars begun to openly discuss the book's possible links to goddess worship and ancient fertility myths. Some modern theologians suggest that the poem is simply a celebration of earthly love between men and women, but this I think is still missing the mark. To my mind it is impossible to read the ancient prayers to the goddess and not mark the similarities to *Song of Songs* in tone, language and sentiment. One current scholar speculates that *Song of Songs* may have been designed originally as a performance piece for a fertility festival. If this is the case, the Akitu Festival seems a likely setting for a work about the return of spring in which a female and male character speak to each other of the reawakening of the earth and the immanent fulfillment of desire.

Of course, none of these theories answers the questions of why the compilers of the Old Testament included this piece in the Bible or why subsequent editors and religious leaders were content to keep it there. I do not for a moment suggest that the answer I put forward in this book is the correct one, or that it has irrefutable historical evidence to back it up. What I do know is that far away from the arid dusty wanderings of Abraham and Moses, Jesus and Paul, a place of milk and honey is found. Which of us has not longed in the desert of life for an oasis of waving palms, warm breezes, and a return of spring? *Song of Songs* is no less than the poetic fulfillment of a heart's cry for rebirth, of our selves, our religions, our world. It is the reaching out of the feminine divine, the spirit of passion and creativity, to the transformative power of god.

Dorothy Livesay

She is a masterful, prolific Canadian poet who wrote about life, desire and things of the spirit. She died in 1969.